ARA OF THE GREENSPELL

SYBIL GEDDES

Cover design: Book Cover/Interior Design by the Book Cover Whisperer: openbookdesign.biz

Typesetting: Redwood Tree Publishing

ISBN (ebook): 979-8-218-42818-1

ISBN (paperback): 979-8-218-42817-4

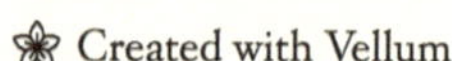 Created with Vellum

This book is dedicated to the memory of
Amy Coseo
1976–2023
Beloved Friend, Soul Sister, Light-Bringer

A NOTE FROM THE AUTHOR

Several years ago, a story began to brew in my mind of a girl waking up in a thick bed of moss. Then one morning in 2018, I opened our front door to find a very large clump of moss in the middle of our doormat. Bewildered, I looked around for where it might have originated.

At the time, we lived in a suburban area outside Philadelphia—there were no shady patches of grass, or large boulders, or other such habitats, for this thick and verdant specimen at my feet.

In the end, I found nothing; the trees were devoid of moss and there was no trace of it on the ground, or the porch, nor anywhere else I searched. I brought the moss inside, placed it carefully on a side table in the hall and went on my way to dance class.

But even as I danced that day, I knew the moss was not entirely random—it felt like a summons. I eventually sat down with the moss to listen to what it had to say. It took me a long time to hear its message, much like straining to hear music playing in another dimension. And this is the story...

PROLOGUE

THE KEEPER STOOD IN THE DARKEST CORNER OF THE GREAT Hall of the Citadel, a place where the sun had not shone in many centuries. He stared at the Flame, burning a brilliant blue as it twisted and flowed like a vertical river atop the podium at the center of the Hall. It had been called many names—among them, the Flame of Truth, the Flame of Wisdom. It had burned for who knew how long—perhaps since the dawn of the Earth. But few knew its deeper connections. The Flame was far more than met the eye. The Keeper had been trained in the old ways, the old magic, and he knew.

The muffled sound of footsteps from the other side of the Hall reached his ears, and he waited until they'd faded. The cavernous Great Hall stood empty. Of course, none would question his right, as Keeper of the Flame, to be alone in the Hall at this late hour, but he required complete privacy for what he was about to do. Or almost, he acknowledged to himself, as he felt a thickening of the darkness around him in answer to his silent summons.

The Keeper stepped from the shadows and felt his old friend pull free from his body and stir in the air around him. He walked to within a few feet of the Flame and felt the cool wind billow against his face. He placed his hand in the fire and let the familiar sensation of power and magic sweep through him. He would miss this light dearly. But its time had come to a close.

He turned to face his old friend, now just visible, a tall, gray apparition that stood beside him, as if sharing this moment of contemplation. "Are you certain that you can recreate the exact likeness of this Flame?" he asked it.

The Dark Spirit made a hissing sound like pebbles in the tide. "Yes, I am certain. None will be the wiser. Perhaps the most advanced among the sorry lot that call themselves Scholars—but they are already under your power," said the Dark Spirit, a hint of smugness in Its otherworldly voice.

The Keeper withdrew his hand from the soft caress of the Flame. It had to be done. The connection to the World Tree had to be severed for him to advance his plan. The Dark Spirit had shown him where the World Tree was located. If the Citadel forces could overtake the Tree, they would have total control of the planet—and he would take its sap and receive the gift of everlasting life. But not if the Flame burned with the true light of the Tree itself. His plan needed to advance under cover of darkness and deceit.

"Then do it," he commanded.

The Dark Spirit grew larger beside him. The Keeper knew that it could take on many forms when It was free of his body. And now It became a dark whirlwind with two glowing red eyes at Its center. It lifted from the ground and positioned Itself over the Flame before descending slowly, eating all the light as It smothered the Flame.

The Keeper shuddered. He'd tended the Flame for close to three hundred years, and even though this was his doing, it shocked him nonetheless.

The Dark Spirit spread Itself flat against the podium, circling like a foul wind, and then rose from the base, inch by inch, recreating the illusion of the Flame.

When it was complete, even the Keeper had to gasp in

wonder at the likeness. He stepped closer and placed his hand within the identical blue and gold light. "Remarkable. It even feels cool to the touch."

The Keeper stepped back, and then turned to the Dark Spirit, which had formed Itself into a cloud beside him. "And the water dragon? Is she suitably sealed away in the abandoned hall below the dungeons?" he asked. The Keeper hadn't gone down there himself, but he trusted the Dark Spirit to spin the correct magic for her imprisonment.

"Yes...the turning of the ages will take place not long from now. She will awaken with the rest of the dragons, and find herself trapped," It said. And then It muttered something the Keeper didn't hear clearly. It sounded like It had said something about a girl, but he didn't take heed.

Satisfied with his work, the Keeper strode from the Great Hall, the Dark Spirit trailing in his shadow.

❧   I   ❧

ARA STARED DOWN AT THE CATERPILLAR BETWEEN HER PALMS. It was bright green and looked curious as it explored the small felt pad on her desk. For now, that was its only place to roam around. It had a tiny face, Ara noted, and its legs moved in an interesting sequence, its little feet walking in segments of four. One of its back legs was smaller than the rest—it didn't touch the felt.

A few giggles erupted through the measured calm of the classroom as students attempted to contain their fuzzy charges. Ara cupped her hands around her caterpillar to create a fence. She peered at it for a moment and then decided it was a "he".

Professor Marlowe spoke with her usual briskness: "As you know, in this class we are here to study the powers of the mind. And how the mind can change physical reality, or matter," she began. "Could someone tell me the first principle of our work?" she asked, clearly expecting a quick response, in spite of the fact that each student was busy corralling caterpillars.

"Mind over matter!" volunteered Matthew, a boy near the front of the class. He wore glasses that were too small for him and had an easy smile. Ara liked him and was relieved whenever he chimed in with the correct answers. Ara spoke whenever she was called upon, but then Professor Marlowe would squint at her and say, "Speak up, please!" and Ara would have to repeat herself.

"Indeed. This is basic to our larger studies here as Scholars at The Citadel. And our thoughts—" continued Marlowe.

"—become things!" blurted Matthew, now holding his caterpillar in one hand. A few boys behind Ara chuckled amongst themselves.

Professor Marlowe simply nodded as she began to pace. She had a keen face like a hawk. Ara watched her take in the entire class in one glance and then turn away. "We will begin with a simple exercise involving our caterpillars," the Professor said.

Marlowe paused for a moment as she snatched up a caterpillar that had escaped from someone at the front of the class. It was Hans, Ara saw, as she watched him hold an open palm up to receive it with a whispered, "Thanks!"

Marlowe placed the caterpillar in his hand with a raised eyebrow. "Unlike Hans here, you must pretend your hands are magnets. Focus on the space just above the creature and imagine a grid of lines there, in the air, like graph paper, as I described to you earlier. Once you see the grid, define and set your mental intention—which is to put the wee beast to sleep."

As Marlowe listed off the instructions, Ara watched her caterpillar explore his little world. He could walk well enough it seemed, but he was slow without the help of that hind leg. And he seemed to be listing to the right. Ara frowned to herself; perhaps she could heal him. But it would involve using her feelings and emotions, and that was against the rules. But unfortunately for her, that was still the only way she knew how to help him.

At thirteen, Ara was the youngest healer in her village. People would often bring their pets or farm animals to her family's house for healing. Well, to be fair, they brought them to her grandmother, the village herbalist. She would make them an herbal remedy but let Ara practice her healing abilities on any animal within her care. Ara would sit quietly, her hands laid on the fur or hair of the rabbit, cow, pig or sheep in question, and send healing through her hands. People seemed to think her efforts worked, but she was never sure how she did it. The only word she had for it was what she called her "heart-beam". But that word wouldn't be considered real at the Citadel, and the world of her village was far away from where she now sat.

Professor Marlowe's steely eyes scanned the room as she spoke to a space about a foot over their seated heads. Ara always found that unsettling. She knew Professor Marlowe was a powerful Scholar, but Ara also suspected that she could read her thoughts and feelings as if they were floating outside of her body —not nestled within, where they belonged.

"You have fifteen minutes!" Marlowe added, before turning her attention to a pile of papers at her desk. She sat at her chair and proceeded to read something that almost made her smile. Almost.

Ara felt her resolve strengthen. She had to help him, or at least do her best. It would be like ignoring a cry from a lost kitten or walking past a slender tree smothered by snow and bent to the ground. She decided to take the risk of getting caught. "Ok, let's see what we can do," she whispered to the tiny green head.

Ara gently returned him to the center of her desk and set her hands in position. She imagined the caterpillar snoozing peacefully on her desk. "Time for sleep!" she commanded. She visualized the caterpillar at rest in her palms and sent that image through her hands. Within a few minutes her caterpillar had stopped moving, but she couldn't tell if it was asleep or just dazed.

Ara took a quick look about the room to assess everyone's progress. It appeared about half the class had indeed gotten their caterpillars to sleep, while the other half was still working on it. A piece of paper turned itself over in mid-air above Professor Marlowe's desk then added itself to the pile at her right. Ara had to be quick if she was going to use her heartbeam, even if for just a moment.

She closed her eyes and focused on her heart, letting it get warmer and larger, as she usually did. It felt totally natural but a little scary, too—this was exactly what she wasn't allowed to do here in the Citadel.

When it felt right, she opened her eyes and spoke to the caterpillar in her mind. She told it how beautiful it was, how bright and free. She beamed her love through her hands ever so carefully, in little waves. She peeked up at Professor Marlowe—if she sensed anything amiss, her professor hadn't let on.

Ara gently touched her index finger to the caterpillar's misshapen leg. There...that was it. "*Grow!*" she told it silently, her heartbeam at full power. All of a sudden the misshapen leg of the caterpillar lengthened to its natural size. A little squeal escaped her mouth, and she sat back from her desk.

A few boys looked over at her with raised eyebrows and she heard a grunted "Victory?" from Orin, the boy sitting behind her.

Ara stifled a laugh as she grinned down at her caterpillar, sleeping peacefully, all of its legs now the same length.

A few of her classmates had begun to walk around and were talking amongst themselves. Ara decided she could tell her friend Nat about what had just happened while Professor Marlowe was occupied.

She left her seat with a quick backward glance at Merlin— she'd decided that was the caterpillar's name—and walked up to one of the front rows. They were seated alphabetically, and since Ara didn't have a last name, she sat near the back next to the W section.

Nat turned her head to smile at Ara standing beside her. "I actually got mine to sleep!" she whispered, her fiery eyes flashing.

"Me too! And mine had a leg that was too short—I got it to lengthen!" Ara whispered back.

Nat's mouth hung open for a second. Ara was usually an obedient student and always followed the rules. Between the two of them, Nat was the spunky one. "Really?! You didn't use your heartbeam, did you?!" she exclaimed, and then quieted back down to a whisper.

Ara nodded in response.

"I want to see," Nat announced, following Ara back to her desk.

Ara pointed at Merlin's leg. "I had to try, and it worked!" she whispered. The caterpillar still hadn't moved. Nat leaned over to get a better look.

"Alright, time to wrap things up," Marlowe announced from the front of the class.

"Wow, Ara...I bet you did heal him!" Nat whispered before she left for her seat.

Ara smiled to herself; knowing that Nat believed her felt good. Ara was used to being the only one who saw things and felt things. Sometimes, Nat would ask her, "Did that really happen?" and Ara only had to reply with a firm "yes" for it to be taken as truth.

The rest of the hour passed without incident, and Ara noticed that everyone in her class had been able to get their caterpillars to sleep. That was one of the reasons they were all there in Marlowe's class in the first place. Everyone was good at concentrating and learning quickly. Most had a special skill, such as languages like Nat, or levitating objects, like her friend, Ember. Ara had the healing power of her hands, and sometimes she could see lights around people's heads, something called an "aura". Old Mr. Cochran, the teacher from her village, had mentioned these things in his letter to the Citadel Scholars before she started last year, and Ara was grateful that had somehow been enough to get her in.

The Citadel was the oldest, most renowned university in all of Amethys and home to the Order of the Flame, the resident Scholars. Everyone younger than twenty-one was in the preparatory wing of the university. The youngest students were Ara's age and the oldest in their twenties, or even older. That was how long it took to be raised to the level of a full Scholar. One had to learn mathematics, philosophy, astronomy, literature and advanced psychic skills. Ara hoped in her case that it didn't have to take that long.

Mr. Cochran had attended the Citadel long ago and had made sure she understood the basics before leaving: respect the professors, adhere to the traditions, and do her best, which was what Ara planned on doing. She'd already learned all that she could in the village, and this was the only place for advanced learning. Mr. Cochran had never become a Scholar, but Ara knew that she could do it. Scholars worked hard to understand the mysteries of the universe; they created new sciences as they went, what Mr. Cochran called "new magic". Ara's grandmother and maybe even Ara herself probably practiced the "old magic", but Ara had never heard him say that, exactly.

The bell finally rang, and Professor Marlowe gave some instructions for homework as she walked by with a basket to collect the sleeping caterpillars. Ara dropped Merlin into the basket with a pang of sadness, whispering, "Bye!" to his tiny head. Then she gathered up her small bag and proceeded to leave in the midst of everyone else crowding the door.

Professor Marlowe stopped her just as she neared the threshold. "Ara, please carry the basket to the gardens," she said in an even tone.

So that was her punishment. Ara knew what was coming as she walked back to the large wooden desk. She saw Nat pause at the door and Ara gave her a short wave to let her know not to wait for her.

Professor Marlowe stood and handed her the basket of caterpillars, now awakening from their unnatural slumber. She'd have to be quick to make it down six flights of stairs and across the green.

"Ara, you know well enough that we do not use our hearts or

introduce emotions of any kind into our work. We use our minds, coupled with our understanding of natural law. Everything must be done in a state of calm; emotions are messy and do not follow the laws of physics, Ara," she said. "If you try that again, your marks will suffer. And it is likely you will not be raised to the level of a Scholar," she warned, blinking a few times for emphasis.

"But—I healed his leg! My caterpillar had a leg that was too short and I helped him grow it longer to match the others!" she exclaimed. Ara bit her lips as soon as she finished speaking. Perhaps she shouldn't have said anything.

Professor Marlowe looked her in the eye, her gaze direct. "Isn't that unusual... If you've created such a powerful bond, then please locate him again," she said.

Ara hesitated to put down the basket. She'd have a hard time finding him in the mass of squirming caterpillars. And how could she prove to Marlowe that it had been real?

Ara glanced up at Marlowe to confirm she was serious, and then placed the basket on the nearest desk. She did her best to quell her emotions and quiet her mind, as she'd been taught to do countless times. Of course it didn't help having Marlowe standing right in front of her, waiting.

Ara briefly closed her eyes and then opened them again, focusing solely on the caterpillars. First, she took them in as group—they were waking up one by one, rolling over onto their stomachs from their backs. "*Where are you?*" she asked.

Ara let her mind go almost blank as she waited.

A few seconds passed.

And then more. She felt Marlowe shift position in impatience.

"There!" Ara cried, seeing a thin golden light around her caterpillar.

She reached out a hand to scoop him up. He seemed to look like all of the others, but his face was different. And he had a tiny diamond-shaped design on his back, and there was his new leg, just as she had seen it minutes ago!

Ara turned to Marlowe and held out her caterpillar. "It's this one..." she said, a hint of triumph in her voice.

Marlowe peered into her hand and then up at her eyes. Ara watched as a thought seemed to pass over her face—for a split second she knew Marlowe believed her. And then she nodded to herself and went back to being the same old Marlowe.

"I do not doubt that this is indeed your caterpillar, but there is no proof that you did what you claim to have done. As your teacher, I am charged with your proper training, not to encourage you to try things willy-nilly," she said, folding her arms.

Ara sighed. She understood the rules perfectly well, and she also knew they were wrong. But of course she didn't have an argument as to why, and professors like Marlowe had most likely hundreds of books in the library and thousands of years to back up their principles.

"I understand," she lied, in a high, quiet voice. She refrained from saying anything more about the tiny leg rejuvenating before her eyes.

"All right—" Marlowe began.

Ara picked up the basket once more. That part of her punishment hadn't started yet.

"—best be on your way!" said a satisfied Marlowe to Ara's back as she scurried out the door, clutching the basket at arm's length.

This was going to be tricky. Ara quickened her pace to fast tiny steps so as not to jostle the basket. She knew the ins and outs of the Citadel corridors and back passageways pretty well, and there was no way she wasn't going to encounter someone on her trip to the gardens. She steeled herself for smug remarks and haughty glances and kept to the side of the wide stone corridors.

Few living things were allowed within the walls of the Citadel in the first place, since the Order largely looked down upon the untamed and unruly. The natural world was supposed to stay where it belonged—outside the Citadel. Even seedlings and little plants were discouraged outside of the gardens, as Ara had discovered multiple times while trying to grow things in her room. Cats were allowed to control the mouse population, and their numbers were kept low.

She passed a group of older girls whispering in the center of the first set of stairs.

"Eew, that is so gross!" said the first one who noticed her. They wore the same long white robes with long sleeves as Ara, but while her sash was white, theirs were blue. That meant they were at least in their third year. Ara noted that the school uniform looked like dresses on them, but more like an overcoat on her.

Ara kept walking, as she felt her own sash loosen from around her waist. She could ask sweet Jana, her dormitory matron, to hem it for her again; she always made sure that Ara had everything she needed. Ara didn't look back but could hear the girls' squeals bounce down the stairs with her.

Another flight down, she encountered two professors walking briskly—they hardly noticed her, even as a caterpillar fell at their feet. She barely had time to set the basket down, retie her sash, and scoop up the escaped caterpillar before it could be stepped upon.

Some moments later, breathing heavily, Ara passed out of a side door and into the light of a bright May morning. *Phew!* Now the caterpillars could fall anywhere, and she wouldn't feel responsible for their peril. All the same, she proceeded to walk along the edge of the green, past the stables, past the flower and herb gardens, to the mulching piles of the overgrown kitchen gardens. Here, she gently tipped the basket on its side to let the caterpillars crawl out. She could come back after her kitchen chores to retrieve it.

Ara spotted her caterpillar making his way through the pile. "Bye, Merlin—have fun exploring!" she said to him.

Hands free, Ara looked back at the hulking structure she'd just left, shielding her eyes from the sun. The white stone walls of the massive building crested the top of the hill. The Citadel encompassed libraries, laboratories, classrooms, dining halls and living quarters for professors, students, and staff. Vast like a castle and intricate like a maze, it even extended underground into the mountain. Ara had only been as deep as the storerooms below the kitchens, but she'd heard the Citadel went much deeper.

The Citadel seemed to take on a different shape from each angle; from the lower lawns it looked like a sleeping giant and from the City, like a fortress. Ara often wondered what it looked like from above. On the side opposite from where Ara stood, lay the Citadel City—a bustling metropolis, home to several thousand people. And on the other side, just beyond the Citadel grounds, stood the Great Boreal Forest.

She could still remember that heady mixture of joy, excitement, and terror when she first rounded the bend in the road that meandered with the flow of the River Embla, a five-day journey from her village. Her father had walked beside her the entire way, as she rode their fat pony, Ginger, her legs swaying back and forth over the pony's bulging belly. Her mother had needed to stay home and tend their large herd of sheep—they had over sixty—and so the two of them had journeyed together.

At last, a small mountain had risen to meet them from the surrounding fields and forest. Her father had stopped to look at the great white walls of the Citadel and reached for her hand on the reins. She'd grabbed his hand knowing it would be there. And when they both tore their eyes from the building, she'd looked into his eyes, misty with tears.

"Well, at least you won't get lost!" he'd joked.

Ara had blinked rapidly and squeezed his hand harder. Her father had wiped his eyes and changed tack. "You know how proud we are of you, chickadee. No one from our corner of the Great Boreal Forest has ventured here in a long time, and that changes with you. It's time for you to learn the new ways, and then you can teach us!" he declared with a wistful smile.

"Don't worry, Dad... I'll do my best," she'd said, smiling back.

Ara was eager to learn more of everything. Her grandmother had taught her how to treat bruises, fevers, rashes, indigestion, and things like that. And she'd learned basic academics from Mr. Cochran. She wasn't sure if she wanted to be an astronomer, or a better healer with the help of the advanced mental powers she'd acquire. She'd learned in her first year that healing wasn't taught as a class, but that was perhaps to be expected, she'd decided.

Ara had then leaned down from the saddle and given her father a big hug. Ara knew that it wasn't easy for her parents to send her to the Citadel, in more ways than one. They had limited means, and they didn't want her to be so far away. Before leaving, she'd spent lots of time with her mother who'd made her a special quilt for her bed at school to keep her from feeling homesick. But both parents had insisted it was worth whatever sacrifices they needed to make.

Ara had closed her eyes in her father's embrace. He might not be like everyone else's dad, spending months at a time in the forest tracking deer; but he loved her more than anything in the universe. That's what both of her parents always said before tucking her into bed when she was little. And she knew they still meant it.

"I bet you'll know the place as well as the forest at home within no time," her father had said with a nod to the sheer size of the building as he pulled away.

Ara gazed up at the Citadel and then back to him, one eyebrow raised.

"You'll see—you'll be the first junior tour guide," he'd joked. Ara laughed at the absurdity.

Her father reached up a hand to replace the shawl that had slipped off her shoulders. Then he pointed to her necklace and motioned for her to tuck it away. A round red stone with a tree engraved on the front, it had been passed down through her family for generations. It was a gift from her grandmother and had belonged to her grandmother before. Her grandmother said it was an illustration of the World Tree, and Ara had always believed her. Smooth and weathered, the talisman looked ancient, and nestled comfortably at her chest. "Right," she said, and tucked it beneath her sweater. It was just the sort of thing that the Scholars of the Citadel might look down upon.

"Who knows—maybe you'll be making suggestions to the Scholars. Don't forget, it's also the seat of government. They make the rules for all the land. I'm not so sure they remember there are people still living in the forest. You'll be a reminder," he added under his breath. And then he turned to her with a smile and cocked brow before pulling on Ginger's reins once more.

Ara turned from the Citadel and set out for her favorite tree at the edge of the grounds. It was just far enough into the forest to be hidden, but close enough that she could easily pretend she'd just been in the gardens, or looking for a paper that had blown away.

Students weren't allowed in the forest—it was too dangerous, due to the threat of Shadow Storms. Shadow Storms were described to Ara as a "dark wind", created from the old magic of ancient Scholars. From all accounts she'd heard, they sounded large but fast, running amok in the trees and leaving them bare of leaves. Ara had never heard of them before coming to the Citadel. They didn't seem to exist anywhere else in the forest as far as she knew, but she'd be cautious all the same.

Ara scanned the grounds for the nearest guard and sighed in relief when she saw it was Henry. He was the nicest Citadel guard by far. He'd caught her napping in the stables once, and he' let her snoop about in the library wherever she liked. It wouldn't be terrible if Henry saw her, but she'd try not to be seen.

Ara had grown up like a feral cat in the forest near her home, making herself forts out of fallen branches and climbing the tallest trees. During the summer, she liked to bring her lunch to a great pine that grew near their old stone cottage. Ara would climb to her special spot and dangle her feet as she ate, one hand on the pine's gnarled bark to keep her balance. She'd watch for sudden bird flight, and the rustling of undergrowth signifying a bear or large animal.

While Henry was looking the other way, Ara slipped into the forest. She had a few minutes before her kitchen chores, and she wanted to be alone. She let out a happy sigh as she breathed in the sharp spring air all around scented with new leaves and damp soil. She took in the webbed ceiling of green and gold above her with its infinite patterns of branches, and the new shoots of ferns at her feet. She could easily imagine a mirror world of roots identical to the arching branches above.

Ara greeted the stately old oak like a friend and placed her forehead on its trunk. This one was large, a Guardian Tree. Some people in her village called them Shepherds of the Forest. The oak grew at the top a gentle slope, the surrounding trees in an arc below. Ara noted its new, bright green leaves, still curled and tender, just bursting high above in its branches. Of course it had new growth—she hadn't been here in over a week.

Ara took another look around to confirm she was alone, and lay down on the cool forest floor, head nestled in between the roots at the base of the tree. The nook was the perfect size for her head.

She breathed in deeply and felt her entire body relax, as dappled sun poured down through the leaves and her body lengthened to match the twining roots all around. Something within her head expanded and her skin came alive; then her edges seemed to go blurry. Ara felt the oak at her head reaching up to the sun. She breathed out and let herself expand along with it. Somehow, it always felt like she could really be herself in the forest.

Ara squinted up at the sky and saw a ball of golden light surrounded by two smaller orbs, one green and one violet, floating just off the ground to her right. She stopped breathing and stayed perfectly still while the lights bobbed and danced at the edges of her vision. Ara blinked to stop her eyes from tearing over and brought herself up onto her elbows. In a flash, the lights zipped past her, disappearing deeper into the forest. Ara flipped over onto her stomach to see them better, but they had vanished.

Ara sat up and looked around. The gray and brown trunks of the trees stared back at her, the spaces between them empty. She walked a short distance in the direction the orbs had flown. She peered far into the trees but only saw the slope of a hill in the distance, and maybe some boulders. What were they?

The sound of bells jangled in her ears, calling her back to the Citadel. Ara brushed off the leaves and moss and whatever else might be in her hair and set off in the direction of the bell.

When she'd made it back to the edge of the lawn, she lingered behind a tree wide enough to hide her. A few professors were out now, walking about the green. She checked Henry's position—he hadn't moved—and waited until the right moment to dart to the nearest gardening shed. From there it was easy to make her way to the kitchens, another figure in a white robe, bobbing in a sea of green.

❦　2　❦

ARA ENTERED THE CITADEL LIKE A MOUSE CRAWLING INTO A gap in a stone wall. She pulled on a weathered door, entered a wide corridor, and made her way to a row of gleaming copper basins. The sounds of people yelling and plates clattering drifted around the corner. The kitchens were a place of happy chaos that often jarred with the hallowed quiet above. Ara looked at her reflection in a small round mirror hanging above the sinks and covered her head with a kerchief, leaving a little gap at her ears so she could hear properly.

Ara worked in the kitchens nearly every day to help pay for her tuition at the Citadel. She didn't think of her time amidst the many chef, maids, and delivery folk; the heaps of apples and wheels of cheese, the busyness of pots and pans, as a chore. She delighted in helping and generally being underfoot, as she would have been at home in her grandmother's kitchen—its size was a mere fraction of the Citadel's.

"If it isn't herself, the fae!" called out Geera, the head chef, as Ara walked into warm air that smelled of fresh bread.

Ara beamed at Geera, who did her best to be a mother to everyone who would let her.

"You can go chop these veggies here," Geera said, motioning to a basket of onions and carrots.

Ara grabbed the basket and headed for the row of cutting boards, nearly all in use by a group of young kitchen maids in full gossip. They paused and smiled as she sidled into position, then continued their discussion.

"I think he's just too strange!" said Annette, a tall girl who lived in the Citadel City, as did most of the girls. "He just walks around, like this—" she imitated a dazed expression—"and you never know what he's actually seeing!" she exclaimed.

Ara's stomach shifted. Did they have to talk about the Keeper? No one really liked him. Ara listened to Annette describe picking up a tray from the faculty lounge and passing him by chance in the Hall. So that's what this was all about.

"I've heard that he doesn't eat or sleep. He just looms about and does those mind exercises," said Ellie, with a quick glance at Ara for confirmation. Ara kept her focus on the carrots. "I know that's not it, though; it's more complicated a word than that," Ellie added.

Ara suspected that Ellie meant meditation, but she could also be referring to the Keeper's powerful psychic abilities. Like all of the Scholars, he could move objects with his mind and that did involve mental exercise.

"You mean—" Ara began, but Ellie didn't hear her and continued on.

"He's just too odd!" she concluded.

Ara returned her gaze to the carrot and breathed a sigh of relief when the conversation took a turn to the late Spring Festival, only a few days away. The entire Citadel City celebrated the coming of warmer weather with a giant parade, and several of the girls would help with decorations. Then Ara could take part as she usually did—suggesting which flowers and plants to use where.

When she was done, Ara brought her bowl to a large workbench near the stoves, laden with soup pots and set out to find the broom. For the next hour she collected dirty dishes, swept the floor and organized the cutlery to be taken upstairs for afternoon refreshments in the faculty lounge. Then she helped herself to a big chunk of crusty bread, a bowl of the fish stew simmering on the stove, and climbed up to her favorite perch: a rounded window seat hewn into the massive stone walls.

Ara sat crossed-legged, enjoying every bite. The lunch hour was nearly over, and she would miss it completely if she set out for the dining halls now, and the stew was one of her unexpected favorites.

Buster, one of the kitchen cats, jumped up to the nook as she was taking her last few bites of bread swirled in stew. Rubbing his cheek on her knee he purred and did his best to ask for a treat.

"Ok, here's a little bit for you," Ara said, offering him a few tiny flecks of fish from her finger. Buster lapped them up and deepened his purr. He was a gray tabby with white paws and a white blaze on his forehead.

Moving aside her bowl, Ara nestled closer to Buster and put her forehead against his. She knew that forehead to forehead meant 'family' to cats. Ara had just started to ask him a question with her mind—"*When was the last time you went hunting outside?*" —when Geera interrupted her.

"Next you'll be telling us what he's thinking—at this hour, of his next meal, no doubt. That cat is too fat for his own good!" exclaimed Geera with a cocked eyebrow. She tossed flour and kneaded a great ball of dough in the same beat. A few of the kitchen maids giggled.

Before Ara could pull her forehead away in embarrassment, she saw a flash of the cat standing on moonlit grass. She tucked the image away, happy that he was able to come and go as he pleased. Animals didn't speak in words, but sometimes they showed her pictures. Buster then blinked at her in his placid way as if to say, "*Until we meet again*," and she gave him a good ear scratch.

Ara slid down from the nook and brought her dishes to the wash basin. Before leaving, she lingered in the center of the room, hoping Geera would notice her.

Geera looked up from kneading the ball of dough. "Ara, dear, come over here," she said in a softer tone, and beckoned her with a little wave of her floury hands.

Ara followed Geera to a quiet corner, her spirits lifting when she saw the rows of cooling racks. Geera often gave her treats, and on occasion, heartfelt hugs when she felt certain no one was around.

While Geera looked for a suitably misshapen raspberry tart, Ara debated telling her about the three balls of light in the forest. Geera went in regularly at this time of year to collect mushrooms. And it was easier to ask Geera questions with her back turned.

"Geera, have you noticed anything odd in the Great Boreal Forest recently? Like when you go to forage?" she blurted.

Geera turned around, holding out the chosen tart which Ara gratefully accepted. It was still warm. Clearly surprised by the question, Geera blinked for a few moments. "Hmmm, well...I can't say I've noticed anything of late, but I am careful. I've seen what's left after Shadow Storms—with the leaves of the trees all blackened and dying," Geera said softly. She fingered a cream-colored amulet around her wrist. "Thank goodness for this! It's from the Keeper himself. Wards off any unwanted spirits," she said. "And I suppose having a guard follow me about doesn't hurt, either. Though I don't need babysitting," Geera muttered.

Ara peered at the amulet before it disappeared under her long, full sleeves. It had the Citadel's emblem of the Flame upon it in brilliant blues.

Ara hesitated, then pulled out her necklace from beneath her robe. "I have something like that too—it's a talisman of the World Tree. It's not for protection, I don't think. My grand-mother gave it to me," she said.

Geera squinted at it. "Oh, now isn't that lovely," she replied.

"Last time I was in the forest with some of the girls we found a great deal of early spring mushrooms: morels and the like. I never know where we'll find them! Thankfully they were all growing together along a little bank. I suppose that was a bit unusual, but it happens," she said. And then she fixed Ara with a more pointed look. "And why are you asking?! I take it you've been traipsing about in the forest? Not alone, I hope!" she said, concern clouding her face.

Ara took a bite of the warm tart to delay her response and kicked herself for not thinking of a clear answer before she had asked the question. "Well...sometimes," she said. It was difficult for her to lie. "But only now and then when I need to get away from here... And really, I was just curious," she added, in what she hoped was a casual manner. Ara could feel Geera's discomfort building and knew she didn't have time for a proper scolding with the lunch hour quickly approaching.

Before Geera could add anything more, Ara darted away with a, "Don't worry, and thanks, Geera!" and found her way through the bustle once more, adept at ducking out of the way of heavily laden trays and pitchers of water balanced just so.

The warmth and light of the kitchens faded as she stepped into the long stone corridor, the air cool on her skin. Her eyes adjusted quickly like they always did, and she took off for the stairs, feet gliding silently on the well-worn stones. The walls were a golden honey color, softer than the blinding white marble of the upper levels. She nibbled away at the tart and let her free hand graze the wall as she walked. She couldn't explain why she felt so comfortable down there; perhaps it was old magic, baked into the stones.

Tart dispatched, Ara wiped her hands on her robe and tried to remember how many junctions she'd passed since leaving the kitchens. *Four?* Counting the crossings on her way to the central stairs lessened the likelihood of getting lost. She'd just turned right at the fifth when she nearly collided with two older boys.

"Whoa!" said the first one, a tall boy with dark hair, hands upraised to ward off impact.

"Easy!" said the other one in unison, with a smirk.

They had blue sashes like the older girls on the stairs and looked to be teenagers. She noticed that they both wore their hair in the newest popular style which somehow reminded her of lily pads. Their bangs were at funny angles to their foreheads, held in place with a shiny substance.

"Oops, sorry!" Ara said, and moved aside, even though it wasn't anyone's fault.

She heard the second one comment from down the hall, "They let children in here now?" coaxing a grunt from the first.

Ara shot a withering glance at their backs and took another two steps before it dawned on her—the Viewing of the Flame! Her class had a private audience with the Keeper in the Great Hall. If she hadn't lingered in the kitchens after her chores she would have been summoned with everyone else in her class from the library.

In a flash, she was down the hallway and heading for the stairs, which she took three at a time, robe flying. She paused outside the Great Hall a few moments later and looked for the right hiding spot that would let her see inside. Sliding behind an open bronze door, she peered into the vastness of the central Hall through the gap at the hinges. Ara didn't want to be late. She wasn't used to getting into actual trouble and had no intention of having it happen twice in one day. Once with Professor Marlowe was enough.

Her eyes swept the pools of light dappling the floor from the lace-like ceiling of marble and mother of pearl. Ara breathed a sigh of relief as she saw her class, still making its way to the raised podium in the center. She went to smooth her hair and realized she was still wearing her kitchen kerchief, which she quickly removed and stuffed in a pocket.

Professor Sai saw her approach and welcomed her with a little wave. The young teacher of literature had a regal but easy manner and more importantly, Ara loved to listen to her read poetry. Ara shot her a quick smile in apology, and joined her friend Nat. They exchanged a look that conveyed they'd catch up later and kept walking.

Drawing to one side of the podium, the small group paused, waiting to be acknowledged. A heavy silence stretched up to the vaulted ceiling far over their heads, and before them, on a raised circular platform, burned the Flame of Truth.

Ara stared at the beautiful blue light, flowing continuously like a fountain. She squinted at it for several seconds. She closed her eyes and opened them. Something was different about the Flame. She studied its very edges, where the fire met the air. What had changed?

Slightly off to the side, the Keeper of the Flame stood unmoving in contemplation as he waited for them to settle. When the Hall was sufficiently silent, he turned to them and held out a hand. "Welcome to you all. Thank you for joining me today, for our yearly time together with the Flame of Truth..." he began.

Once a year, near term's end, the Keeper extolled the virtues of the Flame, and transmitted the history of the Citadel in tones that demanded reverence. The Keeper had large, electric eyes set in a chiseled face. *What color are they?* Ara wondered idly. She'd never been able to hold his gaze long enough to discover the answer. She remembered hearing someone say that he had an "ageless" face. Watching him now, she thought she understood what that meant. Power crackled all around him. Ara often saw glints of lights over his head, and today they were silver and gray like a thunderstorm. Ara didn't want to be mesmerized by his gaze and so she focused on the lights, and his hands. He began to pace like a panther before the Flame.

"Pristine. Everlasting. The light that casts no shadows. This Flame of Truth is the heart of the Citadel, and as such the very heart of Amethys," intoned the Keeper, in a soft, deep voice.

Ara watched his fingers curl and uncurl in time with his

steps. They'd heard this speech before, about how the Flame activated advanced levels of psychic power in Scholars, and bestowed gifts of wisdom to all that were in its presence. For millennia, Scholars like the current Keeper had tended it with the utmost care.

All eyes followed the Keeper as he mounted the podium, drew back the sleeve of his capacious robes, and placed a large hand into the blue.

Ara inhaled sharply. The light didn't sparkle and move as it had before. She remembered the last time the Keeper had done the same thing, a year before. The light of the Flame had sparkled and bounced off his hand like a prism. Now it looked sluggish and dull, whereas before, it had been lively and bright.

"As you know, only the initiated Scholar can approach the Flame, for although it is quite cool to the touch…"

He paused, turning his hand this way and that in the light. Ara shot a quick glance at Nat to see if she noticed the change, but she dutifully followed the play of light flowing over his hand.

"…it bestows knowledge and responsibilities in equal measure," said the Keeper.

He cleared his throat to begin again while Ara scanned the faces of her classmates. No one seemed to have noticed anything amiss.

"While it is true that the Flame bestows higher knowledge and wisdom to those who are Scholars—it represents the search for Truth for us all, as we advance our understanding of the universe around us. It brings light to the unknown. The Flame has led us forward, past the times of myth and superstition into a most brilliant present; an age of reason. Just think of our advances in gravity, and magnetism, for example."

Ara thought of the flying craft designed by the Order, and the system of glow lamps. The flying craft worked with the magnetic field of the Earth combined with psychic power in some way Ara had yet to understand, and the glow lamps distilled a hidden property of air into light with help from the sun.

The Keeper withdrew his hand with some reluctance and continued, "Our history here at the Citadel stretches far back to the time of myth. From this time we have only stories. And now we have come to understand that the characters or beings in the story may not have been real but were aspects of the natural world described in a compelling and theatrical way. Consider the myths of dragons, for instance."

The Keeper pointed to a glittering dragon on the opposite wall. It was blue and held two columns in its hands. "This dragon represents water. Each dragon was understood to represent an element—air, water, fire or earth. An air dragon in an ancient text may be about our early understanding of cloud formations—not an actual, physical dragon," the Keeper said. He scanned their faces for a general understanding, and then continued.

"From the very first myths, we hear that this Flame is from the same light that glows within the World Tree—the very first tree on Earth; a great tree that connected Earth to the stars. Clearly, trees do not have light within them, and we take this to be a description of their ability to generate fire. And so most Scholars now agree that this Flame was indeed lit from the wood of an ancient, fossilized tree," he said.

But the World Tree is real, Ara thought to herself as she touched the talisman beneath her shirt.

The Keeper praised the powers of the mind and the new magic, and Ara felt herself grow warm with embarrassment. Perhaps if she hadn't used her heartbeam so effectively that morning, she would have been able to shrug it off. But as she stood there in stillness, she felt the need to hide her abilities more than before.

"Though the identity of the Builders remains a mystery...we can continue to learn from their precise understanding of universal laws. The size of this very Hall speaks to their advanced building practices," he continued, with a gesture at the ceiling.

Ara glanced up at the rafters, easily a hundred feet above their heads and wondered that this was still a mystery. Had it been built by magical creatures? Or beings from another world?

Ara searched Nat and Ember's faces and finally got Ember's attention. She gave him a look with raised eyebrows and tilted her head towards the Flame. Ember shrugged but then surprised her a few moments later by raising his hand, his eyes on the Keeper's.

"How come we don't know who the Builders were? Didn't they leave any clues?" Ember suddenly asked.

Ara smiled inwardly. Of course Ember would ask the Keeper a pointed question like that. Ember loved the early myths about magical beings and dragons walking the land. He even wore a dragon's tooth necklace that he'd got at a market in the Citadel City. Ara suspected the tooth had belonged to a bear.

"Why yes, we do have clues. They understood mathematics, and used sophisticated engineering methods, as I said earlier. And they also understood astronomy and the exact placement of stars and planets," the Keeper said. He looked back at Ember with a flat expression, as if that reply were sufficient to answer his question.

As the Keeper droned on, Ara's robe seemed to get tighter and her skin prickled with heat. She played with the dirty hem of her sleeve and traced the shape of a flower with her big toe along the smooth marble floor.

Ara felt a tingle at the back of her neck, like someone was looking at her. She hastened a quick look behind, but no one was there. Next she felt an odd pulling sensation between her shoulder blades as if someone were dragging her backwards across the room. She didn't have time to turn around before the entire room swirled and went black.

In the next moment, Ara found herself looking at the ground and wondered why it was so close. There were feet, and the hems of robes, and in the open space beyond that a long, dark shadow was cast on the floor. She could see tiny lines of pink streaking the marble, and a little smudge, maybe from someone's shoe or a chair. Funny, she'd never noticed the pink before.

As she contemplated these tiny details, she felt herself being lifted from behind. Nat and Professor Sai were on either side of her. All of a sudden, the Great Hall was filled with uncharacteristic noise.

Voices nearby cried out in alarm and one asked, "Can someone get a glass of water?" which was followed by the sound of running feet.

Ara put her hands to her head and came to a sitting position in a pool of bright afternoon light.

"Are you alright?" asked Professor Sai who knelt down beside her, a look of genuine concern on her face.

Ara nodded, eager to put her at ease as she squinted into the anxious eyes of her classmates, still trying to get her bearings. Already, she could feel the familiar creep of embarrassment as everyone stared. And why had she just fallen over backwards?

Ember came around to help her to her feet and leaned in close. "Well, that stopped his history lesson... Are you okay?" he whispered in her ear.

"Yeah, I think so..." Ara whispered back.

She stood up all the way and felt a wave of lightheadedness. Professor Sai grabbed her arm to keep her steady.

"What happened?" asked Ara.

"I believe you fainted. Are you sure you're ok?" asked Professor Sai.

"Yes...sorry about that," she said.

"Well, you should head to the infirmary just to be sure," she said, turning for confirmation to the Keeper, who hadn't moved from his spot at the podium. He studied Ara for a bit longer than she would have liked and gave a small nod.

"Of course. You are all dismissed. And I look forward to seeing each of you again," he said, making a small bow. He stepped down and Ara noted that he walked briskly from the Hall.

Relieved to see him go, Ara brushed off her robe and accepted a glass of water from the outstretched hand of a helpful classmate. It felt cool and refreshing, and she gulped it down.

"Come on, I'll walk you there," Nat said, taking her hand.

"I'm coming too," Ember said. "Someone has to make sure you two don't get lost," he added.

Ara appreciated their offer and let the two of them escort her towards one of the doors. Ember was only partly joking about getting lost—the infirmary was a fair distance from the Great Hall, and nearly everything else of importance, situated next to the herb gardens and the forest.

As they left the main building and crossed the green, Ara was grateful for the fresh air. "Did you guys notice anything weird about the Flame? Did it look the same to you as before?" she asked.

"It looked the same to me. Why?" said Ember with a shrug.

"Me too," added Nat, with a pained expression.

"It looked fake today, like it's not the same Flame!" Ara said.

They were silent for a few moments, and then Ara stopped walking. "And I could have sworn something pulled me backwards. I've never fainted before in my life!"

"That's weird... What do you think it was?" Nat asked.

"I don't know! And could you feel how strange the Keeper was? How he held his hand in the Flame too long? I feel like he's not telling the truth about something..." said Ara with a shiver.

"Yeah, well that's for certain. He definitely knows more than he's telling us," Ember said, looking around the green at the handful of students and professors walking between classes. "Come on—let's keep walking," he urged.

Some minutes later they were greeted at the circular door to the infirmary—or what Ara thought of as the healing rooms—by one of Ara's favorite professors, who simply went by the name Agatha. Long before Ara's time, Agatha had taught plant knowledge and the healing arts, but now they were considered extra-curricular. But even Scholars needed tending for minor ailments, and so the infirmary had persisted, albeit on the fringe. And Ara did her best to squeeze in visits to practice her skills.

Agatha had kind eyes, long white braids and an otherworldly air as she glided between rows of nettle and horsetail tending to her garden. "Have you forgotten something, my dear? You were just here yesterday working on that poultice," she said, taking in the three of them as she held the door ajar, her deep blue robe rustling in the breeze. She peered closer at Ara. "Oh!" she said, and drew her to a nearby chair.

Ara didn't want to admit how good it felt to sit down for a moment.

"You look a bit peaky, my dear," Agatha said, studying Ara's face, her delicate wrist already in her warm and capable hands.

"Agatha, Ara fainted in the Great Hall just now. Can you make sure she's okay?" asked Nat.

"But I feel fine, really," Ara insisted.

Ara watched Ember as he stood quietly, refraining from adding one of his usual quips in favor of looking around the room. It was tightly packed with plants in all of their different stages as they were made into medicines: growing in pots, drying on a clothes line, chopped into jars, suspended in curious oils. Ara was pretty sure he'd never actually been there before.

"I'm okay now... Let me help," said Ara. She started to stand up to make a reviving tea and was stopped by Agatha's grip.

"You'll sit here for a few moments, I'll make the teas, young lady," she said.

As Agatha gathered small bunches of herbs from another room, Ara remembered something from her fainting spell. "There was someone or something else with the Keeper. Maybe beside him. I saw his shadow while I lay on the floor and it was far too long, and dark," Ara cried.

"But the Flame's not supposed to cast shadows! Funny that you noticed a thing like that," Ember said.

"Do you mean he has a ghost with him or something?" Nat asked.

"I don't know...maybe," Ara added, frowning.

At that moment Agatha returned with the tea. She deftly pushed aside Nat and Ember, who'd gone mute at her arrival, and handed a steaming mug to Ara. "Drink this, dear. I've left out the valerian because I'm sure you still have much to do, but I hope you get a good night's rest tonight."

"Thank you, Agatha, I will," Ara promised, taking a careful sip. It was called a tonic, meant to calm nerves without putting you to sleep. She didn't need anything more.

The jangle of bells that marked the hours sounded across the grounds. Nat and Ember turned to each other, and then Ara in her chair.

"I have to be in the library for study period today," Nat said, rolling her eyes.

"It's okay— I'll see you at dinner," said Ara.

Nat turned to leave and Ara watched Ember hover awkwardly before she shooed him towards Nat. The two said their goodbyes to Agatha, who left to tend the gardens, leaving Ara alone.

She let out a sigh and rubbed the back of her head where it had hit the hard stone floor. She'd most likely have a bruise there, but it didn't feel serious. It was the sort of thing she'd already been trained to treat. Ara debated telling Agatha about Merlin as she sipped her tea.

After making her decision, she washed her mug and strode out to look for Agatha. Ara found her barefoot in the garden, a small trowel in her hand. She stopped working as Ara approached, and sat back on her heels.

"Feeling a bit better?" Agatha asked, shielding her eyes from the sun.

"Yes...thanks. I just wanted to tell you that I healed a cater-pillar today—it was so neat!" Ara blurted. Now that she'd said it out loud, it almost sounded silly.

"That's remarkable! Please tell me everything," Agatha said, her gaze warm as Ara described the original exercise, and then touching Merlin's leg. When she finished, Agatha had a broad smile on her face.

"Your hands are a gift, Ara. Thank you so much for sharing this with me; I will treat it as a secret between us. It has been quite some time since I met anyone here as strong as you are in —" Agatha stopped herself from completing the sentence, but Ara knew what she would have said.

The old magic.

She smiled back at Agatha, heart lifting with the knowledge that one more person believed her.

Ara said goodbye and set off across the grounds. The air smelled of rain, and a thick bank of clouds loomed over the Citadel. She spotted a perfect yellow dandelion, like a fallen star on the grass. She thanked the plant for letting her pick its only flower and stuck it behind her ear.

Ara replayed the events of the day in her mind. First the curious lights in the woods, then the strangeness of the Flame, the sensation of being watched, and fainting. No matter how closely she felt into it, nothing became clearer. By the time she made it to her rooms, she had almost convinced herself that it didn't matter.

$\mathscr{K}$ 3 $\mathscr{K}$

THE KEEPER PACED HIS CHAMBERS, WHICH WERE NOT UNLIKE
the design of the Great Hall. Even now, after all of these many
years, he marveled at the beauty of the Citadel's design, suppos-
edly assembled with the help of dragons, demigods and other
high creatures who favored spirals and soaring arches. His position afforded him a large, many-roomed apartment along which
ran an elegant marble terrace. Walking from one room to the
next, the Keeper brought himself in hand and focused on the
present. He couldn't yet shake the events of the morning, and
the strange synchronicity of the girl collapsing.

What did she sense?

He had been given clear instructions. The girl, whoever she
was, had something that the Dark Spirit wanted. And he must
deliver her to It, within the Flame, for a brief moment only. That
was all It needed...

The Keeper suddenly craved air. He strode through the open
glass doors, out onto the terrace. He came to rest as his hands
encompassed the stone balustrade, his gaze sweeping the dense
expanse of the Great Boreal Forest.

From the outside, he looked like a man admiring the view.
But the fear in his eyes told another story. The Keeper opened

his mind and felt the familiar pricking at the back of his neck and along his skin. A chill wind tussled the tops of the trees and circled about his face. He let his old friend speak.

"Why delay? The future calls and I have shown you the location of the World Tree," the Dark Spirit said.

It showed him the familiar images of his power—their power—sweeping forward in waves across the land, of great pillars erupting from the earth. It was a power that could sustain itself, free from the old natural laws. He saw the Citadel as it truly was—a great beacon of energy in a field of competing forces. The Citadel ruled the kingdom of Amethys, ancient and strong, but not yet a real empire as it was meant to be. The Keeper would see to that soon.

The Keeper's muscles tensed as he spoke aloud, unnecessarily, to the voice. "There is no delay; all is in order!"

The Dark Spirit had asked for many things. In contrast to the times of the old magic, when the Keeper himself had been trained, the four elements were all under strict control. No longer could they be combined for the sake of magic. Water ran through the Citadel no more; the crystals, representing the earth element, lay dormant, hidden in darkness on the lower levels. The air element was largely controlled by the Dark Spirit, with which it created Shadow Storms. While a nuisance, they served the useful function of deterring anyone from entering the forest. And the most important fire of all—the Flame—had been extinguished. The Dark Spirit had demanded that the larger cycles of time went unannounced save for the hours, and the seasons. But the twelve-thousand-year eras in which the dragons slept and woke, the turning of the ages of the cosmos were no longer noted.

The Dark Spirit had the ability to be in more than one place at the same time, in the very cells of the Keeper's body, in the Flame, at times running amok in the forest, feeding off the natural world. The girl was the most recent, albeit puzzling, request.

"*She is not whom you think,*" insisted the Dark Spirit.

"Is she not? Well then, who is she?" the Keeper asked.

"*Pity you can't see for yourself,*" It replied. And then It gave a long sigh, as if savoring the Keeper's ignorance.

The Keeper suppressed his anger. It liked to feed off his lower emotions, he knew. And there were times when he let it do just that; but not today. The Dark Spirit muttered something in the air.

"Was that a threat?"

"*Perhaps; if you take it to be, if you linger in cowardice,*" It said.

"Be still!" commanded the Keeper. "I have an army to position at the World Tree," he said, closing his eyes and his mind to any more intrusion. The Keeper could feel the Dark Spirit's displeasure in the silence that followed.

At the sound of the hour, the Keeper strode to the end of the terrace and looked down across the grounds. He watched professors and Scholars cross the green, fools all. He was about to turn away when a small figure in white caught his attention. It darted between trees like a butterfly, stopping here and there. He watched it pick a dandelion and disappear behind the edge of a building, which gave him an idea.

With a deft movement of his hand he placed an invisible tag on the girl. That should keep the Dark Spirit happy for now. It could follow her at will if It chose. He had much bigger issues on his mind.

Later that evening, Ara sat with Nat and Ember at dinner. She'd heard some whispering when she first walked into the dining hall, but it had quickly died down. Her fainting spell would be the hot rumor for a few hours at best.

Their conversation turned to the Spring Festival just a few days away. Ara relayed bits and pieces of what she'd gleaned from the girls in the kitchen. Ember speculated whether or not they should go to the bonfire in the City with the older kids this year.

Before long, they fell into their usual rhythm of chatting and sharing notes, and dinner flowed into study time at the library.

Ara made her way to her room in time for the nine o'clock curfew. She washed up in the vast bathroom with its creaky old plumbing and climbed the last flight of stone steps up to her room in the west tower. She opened the door to a familiar sight —her bed in the corner with the rumpled quilt, a vase of forbidden flowers all wilted save for the new dandelion, her few belongings scattered about the simple furnishings. Jana had tried to help everyone make their rooms as homely as possible, but the rooms themselves seemed to resist their efforts.

Ara crossed the room to close the open window. She drew a deep gulp of air from the night sky and thought about her fainting spell at the Flame. Then she reminded herself of the lights in the forest, and Merlin. She saw the two sets of experiences nearly balanced on a seesaw, one side clouded in darkness, the other light. And both of equal mystery.

She changed into her favorite blue nightgown that had once been a dress and retrieved a battered-looking stuffed deer from under the bed. She turned down all of her glow lamps except for the one in the corner on her dresser. It felt like she needed that one on tonight.

A few hours later, Ara sat up in bed. She couldn't tell if she'd slept at all, but she felt wide awake now, her body thrumming and alert. The clock on her desk read ten minutes after midnight. She pushed aside the covers and put on her robe. She slid her feet into the slippers beside her bed and grabbed the glow lamp from the dresser. Something was calling her down to the Flame, and she had to go now.

Ara opened her door a crack and peered into the hallway. All was dark and still. Ara crept out of her room and down the hall, guided by her lamp. She descended the stairs carefully, listening at the top of each set for any footsteps below, her hand ready to turn off the lamp if needed. But Ara had a feeling that she wouldn't be seen.

At last, she reached one of the side doors to the Great Hall. Was there a guard at the end of the corridor? No, it was a chair. Ara turned off her lamp and ducked through the door.

The Flame burned like a beacon in the darkened Hall. Ara realized that she'd never seen the Flame at night; it was ten times more powerful than in the day yet its light barely penetrated the shadowy corners. With each step closer she became aware of the throbbing darkness above and around her.

As Ara stood before the Flame, she simultaneously knew two things to be true: the Flame was not as it had been before and she was not alone.

Ara got close enough to touch it—not that she dared—and felt the cool billow of air on her face. She closed her eyes for a moment to listen. Without questioning herself, she held out a hand to the blue light. She sent her heartbeam forward. *"Why did you call me?"*

There was only silence.

But then Ara felt a presence beside her.

She turned to see the figure of a woman standing at her side. She was made of violet light and was filmy, like a ghost. The woman kept her gaze on the Flame but spoke aloud to Ara, frozen beside her.

"I have called you here. You see clearly with your inner eyes. The Flame is no more; this one is false," she said in a whisper.

Riveted by the violet light that flowed from her face and body, Ara could only blink at her. She should have been afraid, but she didn't feel the need to run or cry out.

"Who are you?" whispered Ara.

The woman finally tore her eyes from the Flame and Ara

almost fell backwards with the force of her gaze. Her eyes were like stars that had fallen to Earth.

"I am Hesperia, the Guardian of the Flame. I have watched since the beginning; I have borne witness," she replied.

Ara felt every hair on her body stand on end. Hesperia turned her gaze back to the Flame, and Ara could see sadness on her face. "What...what can be done?" she asked.

"It must be lit again. It must rejoin the great net of light. Darkness shall not be permitted to claim this ancient seat for its home," she said.

"But—how?" Ara asked.

"Only the Flaming Seed can rekindle this fire, to join it once more to the World Tree before it is too late. One must go there and return with the seed."

Ara stared at Hesperia in confusion. "You mean, someone has to go to the World Tree, itself?" Ara asked.

Hesperia gave a solemn nod. "Yes, you. You must go there, and bring back the seed that contains the inner light—the inner fire."

"But, surely the Scholars know about this. They must! Are you sure you mean me?" Ara could hear her voice rise. The Citadel was filled with Scholars of great power. They had to know about the Flaming Seed and what to do with it.

The woman held a hand to her lips and then looked behind her, as if someone had just entered the Hall, but Ara couldn't see anyone. She looked to Ara again, a gentler look in her eyes. "This task falls to you, daughter of the old green lineage. It is time to awaken, and remember," she added softly.

Ara placed a hand on her chest over the talisman.

"You will gather to yourself guardians, a teacher, and many allies to help reforge this bond. The teacher lives in the Great Boreal Forest close by. Follow the path of the dragon from the Standing Stones. From there, you will be guided to the Tree," the woman said as her body began to fade.

Ara held out a hand to stop her. "Wait!" she whispered.

But Hesperia had already disappeared into the darkness.

Ara stood very still, afraid to disturb the air around her.

The Flaming Seed.

Her bones echoed with Hesperia's words and Ara felt something unknown stir within her. The World Tree was real, just as the Flame had been real. She had known to come here now, just as she knew she must enter the Great Boreal Forest and find the path.

Ara lingered before the Flame for a few moments more. But when the prickling returned to the back of her neck, Ara knew that she was being watched by a being very different from Hesperia—an entity that preferred to remain hidden in the shadows.

Without waiting any longer, she turned and hurried back to the door. She didn't stop until she'd reached her room once more and collapsed into bed, her lamp still aglow.

$$\text{❆} \quad 4 \quad \text{❆}$$

WHEN ARA AWOKE THE FOLLOWING MORNING, HER SHEETS were half off the bed, and she was tied up in the other half. She'd had a strange dream but couldn't remember the details, although the events of the night before were still clear in her mind. She had to tell Nat and Ember when the time was right, when she knew she wouldn't be overheard. Ara promised herself she would do just that.

She got out of bed, threw open her window and breathed in morning air freshened from a heavy rain. It didn't take long for her to realize that she'd overslept, and after quickly washing up she made her way to her first class with Professor Nirla.

Nirla had quick, penetrating eyes and he sometimes reminded her of a ferret. She had two classes in the same room with him, mathematics and then telepathy. She liked geometry well enough, but was excited when Ember walked in the door for the second class. He was her usual partner and always managed to lighten her mood. Ara was bursting with Hesperia's message but knew she'd have to wait until after class.

Ember sat across from her now, a serious expression on his face as Nirla gave his usual instructions. "Senders—maintain a clear and simple image in your mind. Receivers—create a room with four white walls and a door. When the time is right, open the door."

Ara became aware of Nirla as he began to stroll the classroom, surveying their progress.

"I'm going to send you a message, Ara but just hold still, will you?" asked Ember. He'd been twirling a pencil on his desk with his mind, just out of sight of Professor Nirla.

Someday Ember will be very good at controlling velocraft, Ara thought.

She watched the pencil slow to a stop; she could see that he was trying his best to calm his mind. Ara ceased pulling on her hair and settled down. Ember needed almost complete silence to get out even the simplest word.

"Okay," he whispered. "Sending...now!" he announced.

Ara closed her eyes to mirror his, even though she didn't need to. She could often guess what Ember was about to say to her, which didn't count as real telepathy. As expected, she could feel what he was saying more than hear him. They were beginners, anyway, and had a long way to go until they could speak in full sentences.

"You're thinking of the color blue again," Ara said.

"Wow! So it worked?!" Ember replied, eyes popping open.

"Hmm, sort of," admitted Ara. She didn't have the heart to tell him that it hadn't worked like he thought it had.

Professor Nirla made another circle of the room, calling out instructions to finish up their exercises for the day, "Remember to close off all contact in a clean an efficient manner. Seal off your mind as if you are placing a simple white wall in front of your forehead," he said.

Ara never liked this closing part; it felt so cold and detached. But she could feel the difference once she and Ember did as they were instructed. All of a sudden, it felt like he was sitting farther away from her, even though he hadn't moved. Ara felt better when he raised an eyebrow and stood up in time with the clanging bells in the distance. "Let's get out of here!" he whispered.

Ara quite agreed. She was about to slip through the door behind him when Professor Nirla called her back.

"I hear you had a little incident at the Viewing yesterday. I hope you're feeling better?" he asked. He sat behind a heavy wooden desk that made him look nearly as small as she was.

"Um, yes, I'm feeling fine now, thank you," she said in her most polite voice.

Professor Nirla frowned. "Did you...perceive anything unusual?" he asked.

Ara paused. She knew that Professor Nirla was aware of her ability to see auras and energy. But what exactly was he talking about? Had someone overheard her on the green? She wasn't sure where to begin. Ara respected Professor Nirla's intelligence and squirmed in embarrassment in her little chair opposite. And then she decided to tell him part of the truth.

"Well, yes...the Flame looks different. Like it's fake." Ara swallowed, the moment the words were out of her mouth—she'd said it to an adult now.

Nirla raised his eyebrows but his eyes didn't look surprised. "Is there anything else that you sense?" he asked.

Ara considered telling him about Hesperia but stopped herself. He mustn't know. And there was no way that Ara could mention the feeling of being watched and the Keeper's strangeness.

Nirla studied her closely, and a thick moment of stillness passed between them. His eyes told her that he knew she was withholding something.

In the next moment, he smiled, flapped his robes about and reassured her that the Flame was the same as it had always been, that it was eternal; she understood what that meant of course, and that she needn't worry, or spread any rumors. Ara left the classroom in a sour mood. She hadn't started any rumors!

Ara had some free time before lunch and headed towards the

stables. She tried to go everyday—it was where she felt the most relaxed outside of the forest, where she could think and be herself amidst the familiar scent of horses and hay.

Several minutes later she exited the Citadel and paused for a few seconds in the late-morning light. There weren't any guards stationed that she could see, and if she just walked along the perimeter near the gardens it would look normal enough to anyone watching, she assured herself.

Ara skirted the herb garden and lingered at the forest's edge. Her favorite tree beckoned her closer. *"Over here!"* it seemed to say, as Ara paused to considered. With a quick look around—the green was mostly empty—she ducked inside.

Ara ran to the old oak and placed her hands on the bark. She would wait for the orbs again for just a few minutes. Ara plopped herself down amidst the roots and began to count in her mind. It was the only way she would be able to keep track of time.

Ara had scarcely gotten to twenty when she spotted the golden orb. It travelled low to the ground this time, shedding light on the fallen leaves. Ara held her breath as it came closer and grew brighter. It paused right before her, pulsed its light, and then drifted over her head. Ara flipped around and watched it gradually melt into the tree above. She froze, fingers splayed on the bark.

A flash of golden light surged through her hands, up her arms, and into her heart and a warmth spread though her body. The tingling sensation grew deeper, until her skin felt like something was crawling underneath it. Ara inhaled sharply.

Her skin rippled and Ara gasped as bright green vines burst from beneath her skin, twining their way up her forearms, their leaves translucent like the leaves of early spring, fluttering as they unfurled. Ara looked on in shock as the vines stopped at her wrists. Her mouth was open to scream but no sound came out. The leaves wavered for a few moments, as if dancing in the breeze.

Ara slowly removed her shaking hands from the bark. She

circled her forearms and watched the vine ripple. The throbbing sensation had now been replaced with a buzzing tingle. The leaves seemed to have a life of their own as they danced in the air just above her skin. Ara tapped gently on one of the leaves and realized with an inward shudder that she could almost feel her hand. It was all too strange.

She stared back at the oak tree, quiet and dark. "What is this?!" she hissed to the tree and the orb hidden somewhere within. "What do I do with it?" she cried.

But the tree stayed silent and the orb didn't return.

The air around her felt still, like nothing had happened, except now Ara had vines growing from her wrists! She couldn't go back to the Citadel like this.

Ara recalled the warmth she'd just felt and decided to try communicating with the delicate vines. Maybe they could hear her. "Settle!" she told them in a firm whisper.

As if by magic, the vines flattened to her skin like a tattoo. Ara drew her hands along both arms and felt only her skin, warm and smooth.

"Come alive!" she commanded. And the vines responded, coming out into the air like tendrils sensing sunlight.

Ara held them at eye level and peered more closely. They were clear—what she had taken to be an actual plant was more like a form of light. A wave of understanding washed through her, and with a new confidence she repeated her first command: "Settle!" and the vines lay dormant and flat along her arms. Maybe she could control them, long enough to figure out what they were—and what she was supposed to do with them!

Ara pulled her sleeves down to hide the vines, suddenly thankful that her robe was too big. She'd need to show Nat and Ember soon, but when?

The bell she'd been expecting finally clanged across the green. With a long, searching look at her favorite oak, she turned to leave the forest.

Ara walked through the central arch of the stables and

relaxed a fraction as the happy scent of horses met her nose. Unlike most stables that were usually squat buildings with low-slung roofs, these stables were filled with arches and light. Two younger kids bobbed about between the stalls carrying water pails. A little girl named Opi, with long braids, round cheeks and an easy grin, gave her a quick wave hello and continued out of view around a corner.

Ara grabbed a handful of old carrots from the kitchens that she kept hidden in a little basket and made her rounds, delivering a piece of carrot to each horse. Most were pacing their stalls and looked a bit restless. But it had rained in the night, and maybe they were simply anxious to get out.

At last she came to Thunder. He didn't turn around when she entered, as he usually would. Instead, he stood unmoving with his ears flattened. Ara gave his hind legs a wide berth and sidled in close to the wall. It looked like he was listening to something.

"Thunder...here's a little snack for you!" Ara said, drawing closer.

The giant horse swung his large dark head to regard her from the depths of his curious pupils. He stamped his right front hoof and made a low grunt. Ara approached him with care, proffering the last carrot on her open palm. A shiver swept over his coat and he tossed his head a few times before finally accepting the carrot in his powerful jaws.

Ara carefully stroked his neck. "What is it, Thunder?" she asked in a whisper.

Maybe her presence had already soothed him because he went back to eating hay and ignoring her. But Ara needed his opinion.

Ara carefully rolled up both of her sleeves and held her forearms out for the horse to investigate. "What is this, Thunder? What do you think?" she whispered.

Thunder sniffed along her wrists and arms, and Ara noticed his ears turn forward. He then gave her a little lick, as if tasting salt. "That's a good sign, right?" she asked him.

Ara touched his neck as he left her strange new tattoo and returned to eating hay. Thunder didn't seem perturbed at all. Ara could feel an easygoing warmth through her hands from him. "Okay, I'll try not to worry too much. Maybe Grandma will know what this is," she whispered, giving him one last pat before she squeezed past him out of his stall.

Before she left, Ara looked back at the horses' heads bobbing around in their enclosures. They could feel something too, alright...

But what?

After an uneventful walk across the green Ara opened the side door to the kitchens but continued up to the dining hall. She was just about to sit down with Nat when Professor Nirla and Jana entered the dining hall together.

"In preparation for tomorrow's festivities we both wanted to remind you of the rules," began Professor Nirla. He stood at the front of the room, hands clasped behind his back. "Each class will have a chaperone, and an agreed meeting location as well as meal tent."

Jana nodded, adding, "And we'll have quite the feast, thanks to Geera. And I hear the floats at this year's parade will be extraordinary!"

Professor Nirla continued, unfazed. "For those of us here at the Citadel the Spring Festival will end at dusk, and we expect everyone to be back here for dinner. There will be additional Citadel guards in the City to maintain order, and some stationed at the forest's edge as usual," he said, with a long glance around the room. "And we do hope you enjoy yourselves!" he added, almost as an afterthought, before yielding the floor to Jana. Thankfully, she was able to revive the excitement with her closing remarks.

By that time, Ember had joined Ara and Nat. Once the usual sounds of eating and talking recommenced, he looked around the room before leaning in, a devilish look on his face. "I just heard a rumor—a boy on the top floor spotted a Shadow Storm, right near the grounds! He said it looked like a whirlpool of clouds before it vanished," he whispered.

"Did anyone else see it?" Ara asked.

This was new—no one had reported seeing a Shadow Storm in action, just the remnants of one past, like Geera.

"He seemed certain. And no, he said it was gone before he could get anyone to come and look," Ember replied. Nat shivered.

Ara remembered the stables. "The horses were jumpy just now, like they sensed something," she said.

Maybe the Shadow Storm was related to the Flame, somehow. Ara waited until she was certain no one would hear her. "Last night, I snuck down to see the Flame, alone. And I met a being there, like a ghost. She called herself Hesperia, Guardian of the Flame," she began. She told them of the Flame being false, of the World Tree and the Flaming Seed. She omitted the part about the old green lineage, but included her suspicion of being watched while she stood alone in the Great Hall. When she was done, her friends' eyes were wide, their sandwiches forgotten.

"Seriously?!" whispered Ember.

"Do you think the lady lived in the Flame?" asked Nat.

Ara could tell they believed her. "I think that's where she came from, but I don't know."

"So the Flame is fake, as you thought, and now you need to find a seed at the World Tree and bring it back here?" pressed Ember.

Ara could only nod.

"Hesperia," Nat repeated, like a word of magic.

"So…I wonder who put out the Flame," Ember mused.

"I've been wondering that too," Ara replied, though she had an inkling.

"I've never heard of a Flaming Seed!" whispered Nat.

Ara shook her head. "Nor have I. And I have no idea how to get it—maybe it's attached to the Tree?!"

They discussed the possibilities for several minutes while Ara kept a careful eye on their surroundings. Thankfully, their corner of the dining hall was still unoccupied.

"I need your help," Ara began. "I—We—need to find the path Hesperia mentioned, the one that leads to the teacher. It sounds like they'll know what to do next," she said.

Ara prayed that they would agree to go with her into the Great Boreal Forest against the rules, in spite of the threat of Shadow Storms.

"Right after someone spots a Shadow Storm? Are you crazy? No way," whispered Ember.

Ara bit back her retort—that it was all the more reason to go, since there wouldn't be two in the same day—and pulled at her sleeves.

"I don't know, Ara... I'd go if we were one hundred percent sure we wouldn't get caught, but he just said they'll be extra guards around," whispered Nat, motioning to Professor Nirla with her chin.

Ara nodded slowly to herself. They were right—it was very risky. Neither Nat nor Ember felt compelled to enter the forest and find the path. But Ara knew it was more than that, as she traced the green vines on her arms under the table. Something had happened to her. Between Hesperia's words and the mystery of her new markings, she felt different, like a part of her had been dusted and wiped clean. As the conversation turned to the Festival, Ara silently made her decision.

The following morning Ara awoke early. She dressed and made her way quietly to the kitchens first to secure some extra food, grabbing some day-old loaves of bread Geera sometimes left under tea towels free for the taking, and a block of cheese that wouldn't be missed. The kitchens were nearly empty—the heavy cooking had been done the day before and loaded into baskets for picnicking and onto wagons to take to the Citadel City. Ara made sure to take some apples and set off with her stash of food tucked into her bag, along with an extra sweater and her waterskin.

A few of the staff were up, hanging garlands outside the Great Hall. And though it was still early she could hear a band practicing music somewhere.

Ara crept outside and carefully stashed her bag behind the old gardening shed at the edge of the forest. Then she darted back to take her place in the growing mass of students at the gates, ready for the Festival.

Nearly an hour later, Ara stood on a low platform along the long, winding avenue that encircled the Citadel City. There had to be hundreds, if not thousands, of people packed on either side, with more leaning out of windows and looking down from balconies. Above the noise of the crowd, rhythmic drums beat in the distance, followed by blasts from horns as the first floating pavilions made their way down the clogged parade route, hovering at just the right level. Hawkers selling fried sweets and drinks vied for the crowd's attention, adding to the noise.

Standing in a huddle with her classmates, Ara shielded her eyes from the sun as she sought out Jana's face. She'd looked a little harried earlier, as she got everyone into position on the platform and explained the rules. They could walk about in groups of four with an older student or professor; they had to use the buddy system to use the facilities; they were expected to eat lunch with everyone at the large tent just outside the Citadel walls. And they were not to roam about the City after dusk.

"I do that all the time come summer," Ember had said with a snort behind his hand.

Now Jana looked calmer, Ara decided it was time. She felt a little dollop of guilt land in her stomach at the thought of sneaking away from Jana, and then steeled herself. She might not be gone long, and this was the best chance she'd get to explore.

Ara waited until the first float became visible. She saw the Citadel's banners at the front of the procession and then a giant hovering machine came into view. Ara gasped. It was the largest velocraft she'd ever seen. Flowers and lights streamed down from its sides, while people in white robes stood on top, waving to the crowd below.

While everyone around her craned their necks to see the approaching float, Ara pretended to drop something and then made her way easily back to the Citadel steps. With a quick wave at one of the guards, she was in.

The sun blazed down on the white marble steps, each one several feet wide. The grounds looked nearly empty, Ara saw, and paused before one of the many double doors. If she walked all the way around the outside to the gardening shed, it would take too long. She had to go through the Citadel and out the back. Ara chose the closest door and entered without a sound.

Ara blinked for a few moments as her eyes adjusted to the dimmed light of the corridor. If she went past the faculty wing and then down to the kitchen level, she could exit a side door close to the gardens.

Ara took off at her usual brisk pace as the Citadel seemed to loom around her, the silence thicker than usual. As she turned down one hallway, and then the next, and the next without seeing a soul, it felt like the stones themselves were listening, and watching.

She was just at the top of the stairs past the faculty lounge when she heard a noise like a gasp. Someone then cleared their throat and a voice drifted towards her, as she stood with her foot on the top step, hand on the banister.

Ara froze.

"An army in position at the World Tree, sir?" asked a man's voice. It sounded like Professor Nirla. Then came a faint rustle.

"Yes. We have its exact coordinates, and a drill ready to access the inner core."

Ara felt her entire body grow hot. She'd always known the Tree was real, but hearing the Keeper speak about it in such blatant terms shook her nonetheless.

"No more of this waiting and floundering in the backwoods! This will give us planetary control…"

There was a short pause and Ara imagined the Keeper leaning backwards in his chair. His voice sounded like he was smiling as he spoke to Professor Nirla.

"We will hold the tools and the power—of creation itself."

Ara gripped the banister as a wave of foreboding swept through her body. What did they mean about the inner core? What lay inside the tree? Ara thought of Hesperia's words. Was it the original fire they were after, or something else?

Then Ara heard a new rustling noise and a chair move. Her instincts told her to run—as much as she wanted to hear more, she couldn't bear to listen any longer.

She took the steps as fast as she dared and paused at the bottom. The silence had returned; thank goodness they hadn't noticed her presence.

Ara gave her feet permission to fly, not stopping until she entered daylight once more. She made her way more carefully across the lawn and then darted behind the gardening shed. Without pausing to think, lest she change her mind, she slipped on her bag and ran into the forest.

Ara took long strides through ferns and over fallen branches. The Keeper's words rang in her ears and propelled her over fallen logs and through ferns. With each step, Ara grew more certain that the help she needed was in front of her, and not behind.

Noticing her footprints on the soft ground, she wondered how easy they might be to track, and reminded herself to be on the alert for both signs of a Shadow Storm and Citadel guards. The ground rose gently off to the right, where Ara could see the trees thinning ahead. Veering around brambles and thickets of old raspberries, she could make out large gray stones looming at odd angles in the shifting green.

Ara broke into a jog as the stones grew larger and clearer through the swirling green. Still some distance away a clearer picture took shape, and she slowed. Nestled into the side of the hill were stones in the shape of a face, with two large snake-like eyes and a nose. Beneath it there looked to be an indent in the ground, like an animal path. And at the very top stood a circle of stones. Here was the dragon path and the Standing Stones, just as Hesperia had said.

Ara clambered up past the large face of the dragon to the circle and paused outside. She counted twelve large stones, each one perhaps fifteen or twenty feet tall. One was propped against its neighbor and one had fallen to rest on its side. Looking at them made her body feel tingly and strange. For a split second, Ara could see a blue bubble in the air around the circle, like a force field. It reminded her of the golden light she'd seen around Merlin.

Ara took a deep breath and stepped inside. As her feet crossed the threshold, a subtle thrill pulsed through her bones. Her intuition told her that this place contained power, and mystery. Maybe it had been used for ancient rituals.

Ara walked to the far side of the circle and passed just outside to get a view down the hill in the other direction. Something caught her eye on the ground—a large black stain that crept up one corner of the stones. Ara followed the black trail as it seeped from a strange oozing gash on the forest floor, kneeling closer to investigate. It looked like a long, gnarled patch of black knotwood, but unlike knotwood, it was wet. She'd seen knotwood before in old brambles. It looked like a black fungus had eaten half of the plants in a forlorn part of the forest. This was different.

Ara stood up and backed away from the black stain. She noticed then that it extended farther than she'd seen, coloring the tips of branches high above, in a long swath. It had come from above and below. Ara shuddered. It had to be the remains of a Shadow Storm.

Back inside, Ara began to feel the strange tickling at the back of her neck and an inner nudge to get moving. When she was certain she'd left no trace of her existence and most importantly, no tracks, she was ready. She shouldered her bag and checked the sky as a gust of wind lapped her face. The sun was nearly directly overhead nestled amidst strips of white and gray clouds.

The moment she stepped between the stones, the wind whipped at her clothes and sent fallen leaves pin-wheeling in circles around her feet. Ara frantically searched for the path below as the sky above her grew dark and darker still. Shielding her face from something rough that felt like sand, Ara ran down the hill. Soon it would be too dark to see.

A powerful wind knocked Ara to the ground. She rolled into a ball where she landed, shielding her face with her arm. An unnatural shrieking began to build in the air around her. She had to keep moving.

Ara ran as fast as she dared in the darkness as the wind nipped at her heels. All of a sudden, two small lights appeared in the roiling mist, one violet and the other green. Ara could just see them from between half-closed eyelids. They circled and bobbed within arm's reach, and the air looked clearer around them. Ara recognized them as the same lights she'd seen with the orb.

"This way!" spoke a voice from nearby. It was high, but commanding.

Squinting, Ara made her way to the violet and green lights where the storm didn't appear as dark. Ara decided to trust them.

"Almost there!" said another voice, this one slightly lower. Ara didn't question how she could hear them, or why; she wanted to be free of the nightmare darkness that threatened to swallow her completely.

"Only keep going!" called the first voice.

Ara ran, with small encouragements from the green and violet lights to go faster. She scrambled through the brush, feet flying over fallen logs. Tendrils of blackened vines nipped at her ankles, and a kaleidoscope of tunnels fanned around her, ending in empty staircases and moonlit fields.

When Ara next looked up, she saw full light ahead and a

wide-open clearing. Before she could slow down, she'd fallen to her hands and knees on soft grass. Stunned, she flipped to look behind her and saw a thin wall of gray cloud stationed just outside the clearing.

Panting, Ara looked at the great tree in the center of the clearing. It was the largest she'd ever seen—with a thatched-roof cottage, half-in, half-out of the tree, as if it had grown like a shelf mushroom from the side. It looked jumbled but homey with a turret, a rounded central door, something that looked like a catwalk, and Ara noted a chimney and a few rope ladders.

Ara looked back at her hands, and noticed that the violet and green lights had come to rest nearby on the patchwork carpet of moss and fresh spring grass. The two lights gradually faded, until they became a green dragonfly and a violet moth, each one the size of a sparrow. Ara stared at them with a mixture of fear and fascination.

"Thank you! Can you hear me?" Ara asked of the two insects.

Neither one moved.

"*Yes, of course,*" replied the dragonfly. "*And I take it you can hear us as well?*"

Ara sat back on her heels in shock. Normal insects did not respond to questions. And normal insects weren't as large as her hand. This time she understood that the sound wasn't coming from their tiny insect mouths, but somehow flowed into her mind. It was more than just images, like she often received from animals. It was telepathy—real telepathy.

"Yes, I do! I do!" Ara admitted aloud.

"*Thank goodness. We were relying on that. I am Lysander, and this is my sister Petal,*" said the dragonfly.

"*We tried to get your attention before, in the forest. But you didn't follow,*" Petal said.

"*It takes us some time to change states. That's what we were doing,*" Lysander added.

Ara looked at them in awe for a few seconds, then decided to speak normally. "That was horrible... Thank you for leading me through!"

"We've brought you safely here to Old One's house. He'll be back soon and will explain everything," Lysander said.

Ara had a sinking feeling that she'd caused the Shadow Storm —that something had sensed her presence in the circle of Standing Stones. "And who is Old One?" she asked, studying Petal's onyx eyes.

The violet moth shook her wings and walked closer to Ara's hand. *"Old One... A student of the forest,"* she said.

Ara thought it funny to have such a fuzzy and unusual creature say the word "student" but accepted this new piece of information quietly. Perhaps he was the teacher Hesperia had mentioned.

Ara took off her pack and placed it on the moss. Feeling bolder, she stood up, and looked back into the forest. There was no sign of the Shadow Storm. She had no idea how far they'd traveled, but this section of the Great Boreal Forest was ancient. She closed her eyes and reached for the Citadel in her mind and sensed it much farther away. Ara decided she was in no hurry to leave. Drawn back to the treehouse, she began to cross the lawn.

"But—how did you know to find me?" Ara asked of the two, who had already left the grass and taken to the air.

Neither insect responded.

Lysander and Petal circled the great tree, and Ara thought she heard a sound like wind chimes. Ara felt desperate to speak with someone human, someone who could help her understand everything that was happening. She watched Petal peer into a window on the second floor.

A great "caw" rang out across the clearing. Ara looked up to see a giant red hawk circle the tree. She could have sworn it looked directly at her before disappearing out of sight. Within moments the two insects stopped their circling.

"Wait," instructed Petal from the air, before flying after the hawk.

Ara waited anxiously. She had her eyes glued to the round wooden door and the uneven root steps that led up to it. Expecting it to open she jumped as a man strode from behind the tree. Ara let out a little gasp.

Lysander and Petal had landed on the shoulders of a man with brilliant golden eyes and feathers in his long dark braids. Something about his face spoke of great power and great gentleness combined. He approached to within several feet and swiftly dropped to one knee before her while the two insects stayed put on his shoulders.

"Greetings!" he said quietly, his eyes downcast.

Ara thought his voice sounded kind. He fixed her with his golden gaze and stood, while Petal and Lysander fluttered to the ground at his feet. He bowed to her.

"My name is Tobias. My small friends have described their adventures with you so far. I am very glad to meet you. Welcome to my corner of the Great Boreal Forest."

❦ 5 ❦

So this is Old One... He doesn't look that old, thought Ara, as she took in his warm smile. But he did look wise.

Petal and Lysander flew from Tobias and Ara felt them land on her shoulders. Ara saw his golden eyes flash in recognition. Emboldened by the insects, she decided to speak directly. "It's you!" Ara cried. "It has to be... I'm looking for a teacher, someone who can lead me to the World Tree!"

Tobias tilted his head. "The World Tree? Let's slow down. Can you tell me your name, first?"

Chastened, Ara started again. "Yes, I'm Ara. I've just come from the Citadel. And I need to get to the World Tree as fast as possible."

Tobias had gotten up and was walking closer to where Ara stood with her feet planted. Everything Hesperia had said so far had come to pass. His golden eyes softened as he studied her closely.

"Aha," he said. He reached out his hand and made a gesture that looked like he was scooping up a spider off her shoulder without actually touching her, and turned to toss something on the ground. He glared at it for a moment, eyes ablaze, and then looked up at Ara.

"What was *that*?" Ara asked, alarmed.

"You were being tracked. Someone wants to know your whereabouts and I'm afraid I just put an end to that," he said.

Ara had a sinking feeling about being tracked but didn't have a chance to voice her thoughts as Tobias continued on as if nothing had happened.

"Perhaps I can help you. But I need to establish a few things first. Number one, let me see if the Shadow Storm is indeed over. I have just come from scouting it from above and it was quite intense," said Tobias.

He turned away and set out for the edge of the clearing. Ara thought he was about to leave when he stopped to place his hands against a slender tree. He made a symbol with one finger and she saw his mouth move as if he were talking; then he placed his ear against the bark. He didn't move for several moments, and neither did Ara. At last, he turned and strode back to where she stood, the insects at rest on the moss at her feet.

"They say that it's over, and it began when you went into the circle of Standing Stones. I'm afraid you were quite visible to whomever was tracking you," he said.

"You asked the trees about the Shadow Storm? They saw me?!" Ara asked, incredulous.

"Yes, of course. They have a vast intercommunication system. It was easy to learn what I needed. And who would know more about Shadow Storms than the trees themselves?" asked Tobias. "Now on to number two—why must you go the World Tree, Ara? What has happened?"

Ara could see his aura now. It shimmered around his shoulders and over his head, its light golden like his eyes. He had to be the person she was looking for. But she realized that she must sound a bit crazy.

Tobias, or Old One, as the insects had called him watched her peacefully. Ara could feel herself begin to relax in his presence, but she couldn't do that now. She needed action and answers. But what if he didn't know anything about the Citadel, or the Flame? Would he even understand what she was about to tell him?

Ara squared her shoulders and decided that she'd speak the truth. She had a feeling that nothing she could say would shock him. "Okay. Are you aware of the Flame of Truth at the Citadel?" she asked.

Tobias gave her a wan smile. "I am indeed. I was trained there long ago and raised to a full Scholar at a very early age. The Citadel, though, considers me an exile. I call myself a Shaman now," he added.

"Oh..." was all Ara could say.

He was a full Scholar? What had he done to be made an exile? It had to be terrible.

Ara looked at the broad planes of his face. His energy was strong and compact, like he was all in one piece. Something about him was very different from the other Scholars she knew.

"Okay, then maybe you'll understand..."

Ara shared her conviction that something was wrong with the Flame, her fainting spell, and her midnight visitation with Hesperia. She told him all that the Guardian had said and included overhearing the Keeper and Professor Nirla discuss the army at the World Tree.

Tobias only interrupted her once to ask for the name of the Guardian of the Flame and said, "I have seen her as well. This is the confirmation I needed." He began to walk slowly as he listened to Ara describe her escape.

She had just stopped speaking when Lysander floated to her ear. "*Show him your wrists.*" With all that had happened in just the past half-hour, Ara had nearly forgotten. She pulled up the sleeves of her sweater and brandished her forearms in the sun for Tobias to see. "And a tree gave me these!" she declared.

Tobias's eyes widened. He took a step closer and peered at the green ivy snaking up her arms. "Ahh...the Greenspell!" he said in reverence. "This is a rare gift indeed, Ara. I have never seen it—only heard of its power. This is remarkable for someone so young!"

"Well, what is it?" Ara asked, tracing a vine around her wrist.

"My understanding is that you can speak directly to the plants and trees but also communicate with all of life. It is also used to clear spells and send energy. I have no doubt there are more magical properties that you will discover. Tell me how it happened?" he asked.

Ara described her favorite oak and the golden orb. It was hard to fathom it had only been yesterday.

"This gift is no accident. That an ancient magical power should resurface now..." Tobias began, a faraway look in his eyes. "It appears that the Great Unfolding is now at hand. A few days ago, I sensed that something significant had happened at the Citadel, but it is heavily guarded by many spells and my mind couldn't see what it was. The Great Boreal Forest also registered a change. And there have been two Shadow Storms in one day. The Flame has gone out, after all this time and now you are here... It is no coincidence. I feel our time together might be short, but I promise to fulfil my part as best I can," he said.

"Thank you," Ara said, taking in the solemnity of his words. "What is the Great Unfolding?"

"Ah...best to describe it as a change of the ages. We are near the finish of an epoch in which many earth spirits and energies have lain dormant. The dragons will soon awake, and they will reclaim their place as protectors of the Earth. A larger cycle of time is coming to an end. And more specifically, I believe the days of those in power at the Citadel as well."

Ara liked the sound of that. "And what about the dragons? We were told they're just a myth, but now that I've seen that face in the hillside it seems they must be more than that..."

Tobias nodded as if he understood. "The most convenient way to deny their existence. The dragons are most potent elementals. There are cosmic dragons, planetary dragons, dragons of mountains and underground rivers. The dragons sleep and wake in long, several thousand-year cycles, and for much of recent memory they have been sleeping—like animals hibernating in winter. Just because they have not been visible of late doesn't mean they don't exist," he added.

That made sense, Ara thought; there had to be a kernel of truth in all of the myths.

"I'm afraid if all that you've said is true, we don't have much time. You must find the Flaming Seed—a most unusual term, and a mystery to me, I admit. And now I have a duty to stop the Keeper from reaching the World Tree. It appears that a very long life of wielding power is not enough for him. He must also claim the gift of immortality. That's what he wants from the inner core of the Tree—the elixir of life."

Tobias's eyes had begun to smolder as he spoke. Ara felt the gravity of his words pull at her knees—he wanted to live forever?!

"Oh no!" was all she could get out.

Ara felt another piece of the puzzle slide into place, but there were still too many gaps.

Tobias looked at the sun overhead. "I must consult Gobo, and the web," he announced.

Tobias strode to the tree at the center of the clearing and Ara followed. He paused before the massive tree and gestured as if to a person standing nearby. "This is Gobo. He says that he's over two millennia old. He's been my home for many years and I often take his counsel on important matters."

Ara watched as he carefully drew a figure of eight on its side in the air between himself and Gobo's trunk. Then Tobias sat with his back against the tree and closed his eyes.

Ara waited, while Lysander and Petal flew around in Gobo's branches. Tobias still hadn't moved a minute later so she took off her pack and placed it on the ground. Ara rubbed the back of her neck and rolled her shoulders. She took out her waterskin and drank thirstily. Tobias eyes finally popped open.

"What did he say? And what's the infinity symbol for?" Ara asked.

"I'm afraid the Shadow Storms have the unhappy effect of blocking the web to some extent. But Gobo confirms the presence of a large group of humans near the World Tree; it is unclear who they are," Tobias reported. "And as for the symbol, it's a way to begin communication. I am one side of the eight and the tree is the other, and together we meet in the middle," explained Tobias. "But the bearer of the Greenspell won't need that added step," he said. "And Gobo reminded me of perhaps the most important thing of all, Ara: the Greenspell will unlock the portals to the Treeways."

Ara considered his words and realized that she hadn't tested it out yet; there hadn't been time. "And what are the Treeways?" she asked.

"Yes, the Treeways. It is something that the trees themselves have created, spanning the globe; a vast thoroughfare resembling a great forest. You enter through one tree and exit somewhere else through another tree. In this way you can travel vast distances with ease," explained Tobias. "Were I able to visit the World Tree, this is how I would travel; even how I would take you if I could," he said quietly.

"What do you mean?" Ara pressed.

Tobias got up from the ground and looked around the glade. He set his shoulders and addressed Ara with regret in his eyes. "I cannot take you to the World Tree, Ara. You see...I am under the spell of a very dark being. I remain a man as long as I stay in this enclosure..." Tobias gestured to the clearing... "but I become a hawk the moment I leave. And in my hawk form, I cannot travel the Treeways. This spell has afforded me great freedom, but in many ways, I am its captive."

Ara remembered the great hawk that had circled just minutes before. She looked from Tobias to the insects and back. "Well, who did it? And—what can we do?!" she asked, voice rising. Ara was certain he was the teacher Hesperia told her to find, but why couldn't he help her?

"I'm afraid the being that did it is the same that was tracking you, and the one that causes the Shadow Storms. Come, let me make you a cup of tea inside. I see there is much to explain," Tobias said, gesturing towards the door.

"Alright, that sounds good."

She watched Tobias carefully as he climbed the steps and opened the round door. She noticed more feathers that had fallen around his feet. Petal floated to her side and whispered in her ear. "*Old One gentle as a mouse.*"

"Okay..." Ara whispered in response.

Her feet met the soft root stairs and she followed Tobias through the door, flanked by Lysander and Petal. They entered a warm, snug sitting room tiled in reds and greens. The hearth and mantel were made of a purple gemstone, from which a fire sparkled as within a crystal cave. It smelled of dried herbs and wood smoke. Ara took a tentative step forward and placed her bag just inside the door.

Tobias gestured to a seat. "Please sit—you are safe here. But don't take my word or anyone else's for the truth. You must learn to trust your own inner guidance," he said before turning to what Ara guessed was the direction of the kitchen, partially visible down a short passage.

Ara considered his words for a few moments. They sounded like something her father would say. She looked at the still-open door before she shut it gently. Her inner guidance said she was safe, and certainly far safer than she had been in the Shadow Storm.

Ara looked around the cozy space and decided to explore. A large book sat on a stone slab table near the center of the room, surrounded by candles of different heights and a piece of parchment. Beside it stood what looked like a cake stand with a glass dome on the top, but underneath there were many layers of feathers arranged like hands of a clock, long slender crystals, and irregular chunks of black rocks. Something like iron filings surrounded the outside, reminding her of the insides of a pencil. At first it appeared that only a few feathers were moving; Ara thought of them like the second hands of the clock; but then she noticed tiny movements from one of the crystals. A few moments later one of the stones moved itself, pulled by an unseen force.

"Here we are," announced Tobias from the doorway.

He was slightly hunched over, carrying a heavily laden tray. Perhaps he hadn't noticed her snooping. He didn't seem angry, Ara noted, as he took careful steps towards the fire and placed the tray on the table. Then he retreated a few steps away and gestured for her to sit, but Ara was still poised over the cake stand.

"This is really neat! What is it?" she asked.

"A feathervane. It's my own invention, or device," Tobias replied. "I've collected a variety of feathers from my bird friends over the years, and some are aligned to specific magnetic lines of the Earth, or ley lines. You know, birds navigate with magnetism, others are connected to wind patterns. To that I've added some other heavy elements that transmit information from certain stars, effectively tracking our position in space—Altair, Sirius, and others. I'd like to create a better calendar, since the one we are currently using is clearly off by several degrees. But I seem to have other things to attend to," he added.

Ara could see that Tobias wouldn't sit down until she did. She gave the feathervane another glance and returned to the fire.

"Thank you," she said, seating herself on the nearest chair. She gathered a cup of tea and half a sandwich from the tray, hungry from her escape through the storm.

Tobias gave a tiny nod, helped himself to a cup and then sat a short distance away in one of the large chairs.

Ara sipped the peppermint tea and waited. Lysander fluttered his wings and rearranged himself on Tobias's shoulder and Petal came to sit on Ara's knee.

"I will make my part of the story short," he began. "As you might have guessed, I know the Keeper well—indeed, he was my best friend growing up at the Citadel, many years ago. In the year I was raised to full Scholar, he was refused, and a great bitterness grew in him afterwards, souring our friendship. I soon left for a number of quests, all in service to expanding knowledge at the Citadel. When I returned several years later, he was not just a Scholar, but a very powerful one. We were finally able to repair our friendship, and work together. I shared with him all I had learned on my quests, and he took me into his confidence..." Tobias's voice trailed off for a few moments.

Ara peered at him over her teacup. "And then what happened?" she asked.

Tobias pinned her with a piercing look from his golden eyes. "And then came our downfall, Ara. My old friend asked me to go to a place in the Great Boreal Forest, an old circle of stones that had been neglected and unused for centuries. I remember that it had a blasted tree in the center that had been hit by lightning many times. The fire element within it was very strong. He told me that we would open it, awaken it and access the World Tree directly by creating a portal there.

"You see, the Order had guarded the physical location of the Tree secret for centuries. We'd been told it was in a very remote place on Earth, largely inaccessible to humanity, and that it went in and out of the visible world in cycles, just like the dragons' sleep. I thought this was a wonderful idea. I too shared his frustrations at the slow advance of knowledge at the Citadel. The World Tree would reveal so many secrets, and superpowers. In truth, Ara we were greedy, eager to drink from the well of wisdom."

Tobias shifted in his chair and shook his head. "I took his word that we were only accessing the light, but I was very wrong.

He wanted access to energies of both the light and the dark. We struggled to open the portal in the Lightning Tree wide enough, and a Dark Spirit came to us, insisting that it could help. My friend accepted its help on our behalf, and I did not refuse. For a moment I could see the World Tree through the portal, outlined in whitish gold, coming in and out of visibility. It flickered before the Dark Spirit closed the portal we'd all made together. The Dark Spirit then attached itself to my friend. Of course, I did not see this right away. I only discovered it several months later, after he'd changed considerably as it took root within him. This is where the Shadow Storms come from, Ara—the Dark Spirit that lives within my old friend."

"Oh wow…" muttered Ara. "I think I've seen it!" It had to be the eerie presence she'd sensed in the Hall. She told Tobias about the Keeper's unusually long shadow and he nodded slowly.

"And what are Shadow Storms, anyway? I saw strange things in the darkness while these two led me through," she added with a grateful glance over to Petal and Lysander, who now perched on the mantelpiece.

"I'm afraid they're the result of a simple spell in the wrong hands. This Spirit is strong enough to control the air element, blocking the surrounding light and making the wind itself go dark. It can then fashion any illusion or scenes it desires. Its aim is to incite fear and panic in humans, and it kills the vegetation in its path. But otherwise…it's harmless," he said.

That made sense to Ara—now that she'd been in one she could say that they were terrifying, but she hadn't actually been hurt.

"And the Keeper—couldn't anyone tell that there was something wrong with him? That he wasn't just himself anymore?" Ara asked.

"No, Ara. He's far too clever. We both returned to the Citadel, me to my scholarly duties and with his new-found powers he was quickly given the honor of tending the Flame,"

Tobias said. "When I confronted him he turned the Inner Council against me, saying I was the cause of the Shadow Storms because I'd left a portal open for darkness to enter. A very unfortunate lie. This is why nearly all of the portals and gateways to the Treeways and thin places are now closed from lack of use."

Ara marveled at how wrong that was. The Keeper could have stopped the Shadow Storms at any time—they were the work of the Dark Spirit. Tobias was the one trying to help!

"This is why I was made an exile. Not long after that, I was in a fierce and long battle with my old friend and the Dark Spirit that lived within him. It gave him god-like powers and he had given it free rein in the Great Boreal Forest, to feed off its plants and trees. I wanted it gone but he was desperate to protect it, and himself.

"We fought for what felt like days. The Dark Spirit bound me with this spell while the Keeper gave me a mortal wound and left me here in the forest to die. If it weren't for the help of a kind and compassionate Elemental, I would not have survived. She brought me to this tree, and over a period of months nursed me back to health. I never saw her face, just heard the sound of her voice as she offered me direction. Once my body was mended she left, leaving me with this inheritance"—he gestured to the tree—"and a renewed sense of purpose, to maintain the health of the forest as best I can," he said softly.

Tobias got up from his chair to tend the fire. Ara gasped as he stuck his hand into the flames to rearrange a log. "How did you do that?!" she exclaimed.

"Oh—I'm sorry. I'm not used to having an audience for these things," he said sheepishly, sitting back down. "I've mastered the fire element within myself, and so I matched it to the fire here— the two are in harmony," he said simply.

Ara had a feeling this was very old magic indeed. "What are Elementals?" she asked.

"You don't know? I would have thought this would've been covered in your studies at the Citadel, but I fear much has changed. Petal and Lysander are not ordinary insects, as I'm sure you've gathered. They're Elementals," Tobias said. "Nature spirits—the spirits of trees, rivers, flowers, plants. And the spirits of the four elements—earth, fire, water and air. They can appear as lights, or sometimes like apparitions, or in their physical form."

Ara watched Petal and Lysander with a deeper understanding.

"They can take on different forms in different places. But these forms seem to work best in the forest, don't they?" asked Tobias of Petal, who flapped her wings in agreement from the mantel.

Tobias turned away from the fire, his eyes aglow. "Ara—I will not abandon the forest and all of its creatures. I have lived here for nearly three hundred years as a treekeeper, maintaining the forest here as best I can. This is why our small friends call me Old One. Now that the Flame has gone out, this job will be harder. The Dark Spirit will roam unchecked through the forest, and beyond."

Ara thought of her tiny village, and her father even now, somewhere in the woods. Hesperia's words took on a new importance.

"But you yourself are like a key...and the old magic is strong within you. This is why you are such a threat to the Order, Ara; whether they fully know it or not. When you talk to the trees and touch the stones, they will remember; the portals will open... I will show you everything I can, and teach you how to enter the Treeways even if I can't enter with you," Tobias said with steel in his voice.

Ara sat frozen as she took in Tobias's words. A deep knowing stirred within her. It felt like a stone had been dropped in a deep pool of water somewhere inside her, its ripples reverberating outward.

"Here, let me show you on a map," Tobias said, rising from his chair.

Ara watched Tobias gather up the map she'd seen on his desk and unroll it on the ground. She stood behind him as he placed a hand in an upper corner. She could see a white stone depiction of the Citadel at the top near the center. And there was the circle of Standing Stones. There were many trees outlined in gold, but so many other features and symbols she didn't recognize. And the sheer size of the Great Boreal Forest was far greater than she'd ever appreciated.

Tobias crouched over the map, placing smaller books and weights on the edges. He pointed to the trees outlined in gold. "You enter the Treeways through trees like this. Certain trees in this forest are more than trees—they are portals. A place where the visible and invisible worlds overlap—and where they meet. They are doorways, or openings for different beings and energies to move and communicate. The Flame itself is a thin place. And there is such an oak just outside."

Ara felt a tingle go up her spine.

A thin place.

Tobias sat back on his heels and looked up at her warmly. "Now why don't you tell me a bit about yourself. Where's your home and family? How do you like your education at the Citadel?"

It made sense to start at the beginning, Ara decided. "Okay. Well, I'm thirteen and the youngest healer in our village. That's why I was accepted to go to the Citadel in the first place."

Ara described her parents and grandmother, and their home at the edge of the forest. She shared her desire to become a Scholar and her current problem with the rules against using one's heart. Ara decided to share her success with Merlin which made Tobias's eyes sparkle with amusement.

"All of that leading to the magic on your wrists," he said softly. "Do you think you could find your village on this map?"

"I think we live over there, past that bend of the river," Ara announced, leaning closer to touch a faint brown smudge nestled against the green. It looked so small.

Tobias nodded thoughtfully. "A usual four days' journey..." he said, his voice trailing off as he looked at the swath of forest that flanked her home. He nodded to himself and stood to face Ara. "We have little time. Let me show you around and then let's see what the Greenspell has to teach us."

❅ *6* ❅

THE KEEPER LAY IMMOBILE ON HIS BACK, BLINKING UP AT THE distant ceiling. His hands curled and uncurled in a minuscule motion, a faint echo of his earlier habit. He could blink and just barely move his fingers—that was the extent of his movement. He'd been frozen for what felt like an eternity, though he knew less than a few hours had passed, containing many long minutes of communicating his wishes to the staff through blinking.

He heard a movement at the door and then the heavy scrape of the wood on stone. Of course, one of the nurses would have been sent to visit him before midday, which was just as well. His mouth was parched, and though he yearned for food he knew that need would not be met today.

"Eminence, sir, I'm here to check on you," said a gentle female voice.

The Keeper didn't recognize the worried face that hovered above his own. The woman checked his blankets and cradled his head as she administered the water. The Keeper wanted to tell her to give him something a bit stronger, but he could tell she wouldn't follow the code in his blinking pattern. Only Jana had figured that out. As she resettled him, he let a tired sigh escape his lips.

"I'm so sorry, sir. Are you comfortable enough for now? Someone will check on you again in a few hours," she assured him.

The Keeper could feel her discomfort cloying around, and a flash of irritation shot through him. How ridiculous to have his nearly perfect physical body if he couldn't use it properly! He gave two long blinks to signal, "Yes, I'm fine." Thankfully that seemed to appease her, and the worried face floated from the room.

The Dark Spirit had exerted Its power in a wholly new way, a way unfathomable to the Keeper just a day before. He'd stood by the Flame, alone in the absence of students and staff due to the Festival. The Voice had entered as It often did, insisting on prominence, insisting on the girl being delivered.

The Keeper had been about to tell It to settle down when It had come tearing out of the Flame itself. The Keeper had gasped and stumbled backwards. In the next moment he was pushed against the floor with the weight of a few hundred pounds along every inch of his body. The Voice was clear and triumphant in his ears—

"*Are you surprised? Didn't know I could do that, did you?*" it had taunted him. "*Now you will listen, as my friend or servant, whichever you prefer...*"

The Keeper's panic increased as It continued to speak, each word impressing upon him Its mastery of the situation, and the moment, and how very wrong he'd been.

"*You let her escape! And this is your punishment,*" It said in satisfaction, before changing course in the next breath. "*I have doubled your empire and led you to the World Tree. Your army is mere miles away... Such a small thing I have asked for,*" said the Voice with self-pity.

The Keeper knew that wasn't entirely true—It had long used the Flame, and the forest, and his own life essence as food in return. Perhaps the Dark Spirit had suffered slightly from losing Its access to the genuine Flame, but the Keeper doubted its severity. He knew It was always hungry for more—more chaos, more things to devour, more of Its own power. They were intertwined now. As the Keeper grew in power so did the Dark Spirit. But what It said next gave him chills.

"*I have plans of my own now,*" It had said cryptically.

The Dark Spirit had been a part of him for so very long. To hear that It had Its own intentions and schemes was unwelcome news. The Keeper had waited for more but the Voice had gone silent.

"I will find her," he'd promised, through frozen lips.

And then It had left abruptly, as if Its attention had been called somewhere else more important.

The Keeper's mind raced with questions and possibilities—had It returned to the Great Boreal Forest? Or burrowed into the crystal caves far beneath the Hall? And even more disturbing, was It in communication with something larger than he'd realized? Was It only a messenger?

The Keeper lay on the cold stone floor until a guard found him. Soon, he assured himself, he would access the World Tree. And then he would be free of the Dark Spirit once and for all. Now that he'd lived this long, he wouldn't let his one opportunity for everlasting life slip by. And with immortality, he would retain his position of absolute authority.

The Keeper felt an usual sensation gather around his eyes. It would be a few hours longer until he could overpower the Dark Spirit and regain control of his body, he knew. He would need all of his resources to do it successfully without inciting a battle.

With some reluctance, he focused on his heartbeat. He'd already sent orders to have the girl hunted down on foot and the Dark Spirit would be satisfied. Wishing for relief, a few tears tumbled from his eyes down his still-warm cheeks.

Tobias gave Ara a quick tour of the glade, including his beautiful garden that grew in the shape of a flower—something he called a mandala—and an apiary of special bees that spent the winter deep below the earth in a crystal cave. He stood just outside of his garden, arms at his sides, feet planted a few feet apart. Once she had drawn near, he fixed her with a direct look.

"You may have been taught to connect with the magic and the invisible through the mind, but I see that you can do far more. I will teach you how to reconnect to the great net of life— to sense and know in relation to nature. These are all abilities lying within you that just need awakening. Magic is how the invisible realm flows *through* you, Ara, because you are a part of it! To travel the Treeways you need to be able to open the portals in the gateway trees, the ones edged in gold on the map. And to do that you must have a deeper understanding of the web—or what one might call the mycelium," he said. "It might sound complicated, but we'll work slowly, step by step. Alright?" he asked.

Ara nodded; she liked the sound of that. She didn't just want to figure things out on paper, though she liked doing that well enough. But she liked to feel things, too. Like with Merlin the caterpillar. "Are you talking of *old* magic?" she asked.

"I would call it ancient magic. And if I were you, I'd be sure to master both the new and the old," he replied with a glint of mischief in his eyes.

Tobias gestured to the trees in the circle. "What do you notice about these trees along the perimeter?" he asked her.

Ara took a step back and studied the surrounding woods. She pulled on the sleeve of her sweater, as she took in what she could. After several moments, she saw a pattern. "Oh! I didn't see this before. There are all different kinds of trees that don't usually grow together! Like that maple right next to that spruce tree... And they're almost all the same size, like the ones I call guardian trees! Big trees that look after the smaller ones around them," she said, looking to Tobias for confirmation.

"Exactly. And it's interesting that you call them that, for that is what they are. Large trees such as these often grow in the presence of many smaller trees and share resources. The presence of Gobo brought them here, representatives of many species in the forest, deciduous and evergreen. They are living side by side, and even their roots are connected," he said.

Tobias looked to Ara and spread his hands open to include the glade. "Find anywhere comfortable where you can sit and relax," he said.

Ara took her time finding the perfect spot, eventually settling on a place near the center, a mossy patch of grass in the sun. She sat down cross-legged and Tobias brought her some water.

"I want you to sense what you can below the ground, now. Travel a good twelve feet below the earth here with your mind, and get acquainted with the feelings and sensations there. When you are done, come and find me," he said.

"Okay!" Ara agreed.

Tobias gave her a wave and walked off in the direction of the bees.

Once settled, Ara envisioned roots branching down from her feet that travelled just the right distance into the soil below. When it felt like she'd gone twelve feet, she swam down the roots to look around.

Ara had the sensation of darkness and density all around her, like she was encased in mud, or nestled deep in a cave. Eyes closed, she relaxed into the feeling, imagining herself like a tiny seed, coiled and resting. She felt safe and very quiet.

Ara could feel herself almost drift off to sleep as her body above swayed in the sun. After a short time, she decided to explore around her and sent out a tentative feeler into the surrounding soil.

In her mind's eye, she scanned the darkness, and found that it was no longer as dark as it had been. In fact, she could almost make out a net of roots all around her. They reminded her of an after-image from looking at the sun, like a bright violet web that extended in all directions. She could sense movement around her too. A subtle kind of electricity moved through the net, accompanied by myriad pinpricks of light.

Ara reached out her hand to the violet web. It rippled at her touch and then seemed to press against her gently, like an animal taking in her scent. For the first time she became aware of a great low hum all around her, like a song of life in the soil. She knew that as she touched the web it was vibrating through her, radiating out into the glade and all of the forest. This world had been beneath her feet, unconsidered and invisible, her entire life! Ara basked in this sense of mystery and connection, and then returned back to her body once more. Ara opened her eyes and gave her body an instinctual shake.

Tobias stood nearby, a curious expression on his face. "Did you sense the underground web?" he asked gently.

"Yes! I could see it in my mind!" Ara announced, breathless.

Tobias nodded. "The mycelium connects all of the trees together. This was the network I mentioned earlier. It is a vast communication system, governed by electrical impulses, the flow of water, which holds images and information, and of course, nutrients," he concluded.

Ara could only look at him in awe.

"And now let's see what you can do with the Greenspell, Ara," Tobias said as he walked toward a large oak tree. It had clusters of dandelions growing at the base that Ara hadn't noticed before.

"Do the dandelions mean anything special, or are they just growing there?" she asked.

"I'm glad you noticed. Yes, they often grow in places of power. When you see them at the base of an old tree like this, take it as a sign of something special within it," Tobias explained. "Now, why don't you connect to this tree using your hands? See what you can discover on your own."

Ara looked into his golden eyes and then approached the

tree. "Come alive!" she whispered to the Greenspell, and the vines lifted off her skin.

She placed both hands on the oak, fingers spread wide and closed her eyes. An image of the oak tree as a mighty column of light burst into her mind. It was strong, and patient. And it knew who she was somehow.

Ara waited but nothing else happened. She opened her eyes and drew her hands away. She looked to Tobias. "I think I connected!"

He didn't meet her gaze, but peered at the bark until he uttered, "There!" softly.

A golden circle of light appeared faintly in the bark. For a moment it looked like a complex pattern shimmered just beneath the surface until a simple spiral remained, strong and bright. Ara looked in wonder from the golden spiral to Tobias.

"Well done, Ara. You've just revealed its golden markings, or seal," Tobias said.

He put a hand above the spiral and Ara watched it flicker. "You've now completed the first step. To enter the Treeways, you place your hand on the seal. And then comes the more delicate part... You must build yourself a bridge with the help of this tree and its roots. Imagine the bark opening before you, and a pathway just beyond. You can create any kind of path you'd like, but you must see it very clearly in your imagination."

Ara tore her eyes away from the spiral to question Tobias. "Can it look like a regular path, then? Or could it be something unusual, like a light beam?" she asked.

"It could definitely be unusual. You will know it's working when you see your inner vision come to life before you. If you imagine a golden road, or a path of ferns, it will appear on the other side. Try it, Ara!" Tobias said, a glimmer of fire in his eyes.

Ara decided on the path she would create. Taking a step forward, she placed her hands on the seal and closed her eyes. With a clear focus she imagined the bark disappearing to reveal an oval-shaped door. Beyond that, a blue beam of light led into a field of green.

"Keep sending the image—it's working!" Tobias said beside her.

Ara squinted her eyes and strained with the effort of creating the clearest blue path she could imagine and realized that she'd seen a such a light before, in the Flame.

Something shifted beneath her hands.

"Ahh," he finally said.

Ara opened her eyes. Where there had once been solid bark, stood an open oval door, and a bright blue path of light led into what looked like an emerald forest. Ara stuck her head in a few inches— it was a completely different forest from the one she was standing in with Tobias. There at her feet were the remains of fallen leaves and a bed of thick green moss. The air was different on the other side, softer and still. There was full sun, approaching mid-afternoon, but everything seemed to glow.

"Here are the Treeways. It is one thing to describe them, but quite another to experience them for oneself. You have a bit more to learn before entering, so with your permission I will show you how to close your gateway."

Ara gazed with longing at the emerald forest. "Yes, okay... Do you think I can make it again?"

"Certainly." Tobias stepped closer to Ara. "Now ask the tree to close the gateway. Then thank it for giving you permission to enter," he said.

Ara did as instructed and kept repeating her thanks to the tree throughout every step. This time she kept her eyes open as the emerald forest faded, her blue path shortened and the bark resealed itself until only the curled gray lines remained. The tree went back to being a regular oak beneath her hands.

"That is incredible!" she said to Tobias, who now leaned against the side of the tree, arms crossed.

His hands dropped to his sides and a look of wonder crossed his face. His eyes widened as if he'd just remembered something.

"You can awaken the Sleeping Ones with the Greenspell, Ara! The prisoners of the Treeways," he said, with excitement. "I hadn't appreciated this before..."

"The Sleeping Ones? Who are they?" Ara asked.

Tobias had begun his slow, thinking walk. "They are beings from long, long ago—early humans, Elementals, even ordinary people—they're all suspended in a dream state in the Treeways, locked in time. The Treeways are ancient and have been used by the forces of darkness at different times, to travel at will. I suspect the Dark Spirit has used it as well and imprisoned some very powerful beings there. Just the sort of beings who could protect the World Tree from an army. I myself have seen their faces in the trees but did not possess the power to free them from their slumber. But I believe you can," he added, shooting Ara a challenging look. "Let's—"

A distant boom like thunder echoed through the glade, and for a brief moment Gobo shook with the sound. Lysander and Petal flew to Tobias's shoulder as he stood looking into the sky with a dark expression. A hush pervaded the air, and nothing moved in the forest. The sky was still clear but a bank of dark clouds amassed to the north.

Was it another Shadow Storm? Had a tree fallen nearby? It had to have been enormous to make that noise, Ara thought, but it was possible.

Tobias turned his head slightly as if to listen more. Ara drew her hands along her wrists, the Greenspell flat like a tattoo.

"With your permission, I'd like to go and investigate," Tobias said to Ara.

"Okay! Shall I stay here and practice?" she asked.

"*It can't hurt.*" His warm voice seemed to ring clearly in her ears, but his face had remained a mask of calm. Had she just heard him speak? Where was he speaking from?

Ara blinked a few times. "Can you do that again?" she asked timidly.

"*Of course... Can you hear me, Ara?*" he said without moving his mouth.

"Yes! This is like the telepathy we practice—but it's different!" she said in a rush.

"*It is! See if you can respond,*" he said.

Ara gathered up her energy and without much reflection, yelled to Tobias from her mind. "*CAN YOU HEAR ME?!*"

Tobias winced and then shook his head. "Not yelling from your mind, Ara. Try speaking the words lower, from your heart," he said aloud.

It felt like she needed to close her eyes for this first try. Ara did her best to relax and sent a short, simple message through her heart to her most unusual teacher standing opposite. "*Is this better?*" she asked.

"*That's it! And you can still hear me, correct?*"

"*YAY! Yes, yes, I can,*" Ara said, and opened her eyes. She beamed at Tobias.

Tobias shifted his weight and then spoke aloud. "I am very pleased we were able to establish that, Ara! I suspected it was possible and had a feeling it might come in handy. Let's return to normal speech for a while," he said, already turning to leave.

"It's easier than I thought," Ara said, walking in step with Tobias towards Gobo. "We have a class in telepathy, and it's really difficult!" Ara described her limited attempts with Ember.

"Undoubtedly the hard way," added Tobias under his breath. "Everyone can do this already, Ara. It's simply that they've forgotten how," he added at the door. "I won't be long, but I would prefer if you stayed in the tree. Perhaps you can repack your bag for a longer training journey into the Treeways."

"Okay, I'll do that!"

She had a strange feeling about Tobias leaving now, but she pushed it aside. Of course, he needed to see what was happening in the forest. In his bird form he might get a glimpse of what had made the noise.

"Not to worry, Ara. Remain positive," he instructed, as if reading her thoughts. He waved a hand as he walked away.

Ara watched Tobias walk towards the edge of the glade, where he could undergo his change in the forest. Petal and Lysander trailed him for a bit, and Ara could hear a quiet exchange between the three of them before the Elementals returned to Ara's side.

Once inside, Ara busied herself in Tobias's kitchen and spent a few moments lingering over the map of the Great Boreal forest. She'd just counted two golden trees near her village when Lysander and Petal streaked into the room.

"*Men are coming—bolt the door!*" cried Petal.

Ara rushed to the front door and clutched the heavy sliding lock with shaking hands, feeling it slide into position with a metallic thud.

Heart thumping, she ran to the window and positioned herself so she could see without being seen from outside. Petal and Lysander stationed themselves above the window, looking down.

After what felt like a short eternity of waiting, she saw the branches part and three figures walk into the glade. Tobias was flanked to the front and back by two hunters from the Citadel. His face was a solemn mask and one of his arms was covered with feathers, as though his transformation into a hawk had been interrupted.

Ara's jaw dropped as she watched them walk in a quiet procession towards the door. Was Tobias leading them in? Ara searched the faces of the two men dressed in green with powerful builds and the unmistakable mark of the Citadel guard on their vests. They walked stiffly and their faces had a blank expression as they looked around the clearing. Ara didn't recognize either of them. Tobias had his eyes downcast as he walked.

In the next moment they were on the stairs and out of view. Ara heard a loud, unwelcome *thud, thud, thud* on the door.

She remained frozen at her spot by the window.

Thud, thud, thud.

Even the sound rang wrongly in her ears.

This wasn't Tobias. This couldn't be happening.

"Ara, can you hear me? Please, can you hear me?!"

Still afraid to move, Ara let out a short gasp as the familiar unspoken words entered her heart and echoed through her mind.

"Yes, Tobias?! Is it really you?" she sent back in desperation.

"Thank the light... Yes, Ara..." he sent back.

There was another round of thudding at the door, and then he continued: *"We don't have much time. It was a trap, and I have been injured—they knew my weakness in advance—and am using all of my powers to control these two against nature. They will only remember being here, searching for you, and not finding you. I will let them capture me and take me to the Citadel. I see that it is best that I work there from the inside...*

"You now have a choice to make, Ara. You may enter the Treeways safely with the Elementals. Build a bridge to your favorite tree near your home, and they will be able to navigate for you. Or—you can travel to the World Tree. If you choose the latter, tell all of the Elementals you can find that an army from the Citadel aims to capture the World Tree. This is more important than my life, Ara. Which do you choose?"

Ara didn't need to think about it. *"I will do it! I will warn them!"* she replied.

As she spoke the words with her heart, a quiet certainty took shape inside her. There was a slight pause. And then Tobias spoke again.

"When you are ready, you will open the door and run upstairs. Open a window and climb onto a branch. They will search but do not let them see you; climb into the tree if you must! Are you ready?"

She would never be ready, but she would do it.

Ara sidled up close to the door and pulled the bolt soundlessly out of its resting place. Without another look, she sprinted up the stairs into a small bedroom. She had the window open and was already out on the massive branch below when she heard the door to the great tree bang open.

The sounds of chairs and tables being overturned drifted up from below as she looked for the right places for her hands and feet. With heart thudding and tears clouding her vision, Ara began to climb.

Lysander and Petal flew to her side. Without speaking, they helped her climb until she sat in a sturdy crook with a good view of the glade, still hidden amongst the leaves.

At last, the hunters came into view with Tobias between them. He was bound in some way, but Ara couldn't see a rope. The arm with feathers hung limply at his side, wrapped in a kitchen cloth.

"*Oh, Old One...*" whispered Petal.

Ara's heart dropped as Tobias walked without a backward glance between the hunters. And then his voice found her.

"*Brave Ara... Be alert. Darkness still walks the Treeways. Remember that you are not alone. And you will find the Flaming Seed!*" he sent.

"*Tobias! Tobias!*" Ara called.

In the next moment, two men had entered the forest with a giant bird caught between them. Tobias was now a hawk, and their connection broken.

Ara felt the soft pat of moth wings on her arms. She wiped her eyes and blinked into two sets of tiny onyx eyes. She saw tenderness in both.

"*Old One is very strong. He will outsmart them the first chance he gets!*" declared Petal, still patting her hand. "*Maybe he'll enter a tree to escape them?*" she added, eyebrows raised in hope.

Ara felt that Lysander didn't look quite as optimistic, but he didn't speak.

She took a deep breath. It was time to go down and clean the mess the hunters had made in the tree. Ara could tell the Elementals were waiting for her to move—Lysander immediately sprang into action and darted down the tree.

Several minutes later, Ara had tidied the house. She put the broom back in its place in the kitchen and surveyed the sitting room. The feathervane, miraculously intact under its glass bell, drew her over.

Ara peered down at its intricate face. After a few moments of stillness, a small feather moved. Maybe it was one of Tobias's feathers, signaling his journey. She pondered its curious lack of movement for a moment before meeting Petal and Lysander in the sitting room.

"You're safe with us. We will lead you to the World Tree now... Are you ready?" asked Petal.

Ara inclined her head to the moth with a tired smile. "Thank you, Petal... I think I am," she said. Ara heard herself speak the words as if they came from a wiser, deeper self.

In the next moment, the two insects were abuzz. Ara went into the kitchen to repack her bag. This time she added fewer provisions—bread, honey, cheese, and water. She made space for a blanket and her warm sweater.

Lysander flew to the door and gestured for Ara to open it. When her hand met the knob, she revisited the events of the hour before and then turned it with purpose. They were moving forward.

A warm orange glow met their faces as the day approached sunset. The glade felt quiet and soft, as birdsong rippled through the trees.

Standing in the doorway, Ara looked back at the sitting room with an upwelling of gratitude. She walked over to one of the smooth, contoured walls and placed a palm on the golden wood. Ara closed her eyes and sent her message of thanks to the tree as the Greenspell leapt to life on her wrist.

Like a pillar of light, a great being grew near her. Or maybe it was all around her... Ara took a sharp intake of breath at its power and size. It felt immense, much larger than the giant tree itself.

"You have safe passage little one. And I thank you on behalf of all of the forest," he said.

"Thank you, Gobo! I'll do my best," Ara replied, his words making her feel better.

Ara let the feeling of embrace wash through her as the light faded from her inner vision. She opened her eyes and looked at her small hand against the wood. The vines flattened once more and she drew her hand away with a feeling of togetherness. It wasn't just Tobias, herself, or the Elementals fighting against the dark forces.

Ara doused the fire and closed the door to the great tree behind her. She would take the path to the World Tree. She would retrieve the Flaming Seed. And now she would also free Tobias.

"*Over here!*" Petal called to her from beneath the portal oak. Ara joined her and placed her hands on the bark. Willing the Greenspell alive, she tried to remember what she'd felt earlier.

After a few moments, the bark of the oak began to move and shimmer, like a heatwave over a hot roof. It thinned beneath her hands and a space like a window appeared. Ara could see emerald-green light coming from the other side.

The insects circled wildly around her as she completed the final step, a blue path leading to the Treeways.

"*Follow us through!*" Petal called, as she slowed before the window.

Ara squinted into the tree. The opening was just wide enough for her to climb through, reaching from this world to the other.

Petal and Lysander zipped through the portal together, and disappeared into the light.

⚜   7   ⚜

THE SUDDEN CHANGE IN AIR PRESSURE MADE ARA GASP. HER arms tingled and burned and she heard a high-pitched sound that seemed to encircle her head.

In the next moment, she was thrust forward through the opening, landing on her hands and knees. Ara felt a bank of rich moss beneath her hands. Blinking in the light, she got to her feet and looked around.

She stood in an emerald forest that stretched as far as the eye could see. All of the trees were the same size, aligned in endless rows so that everywhere she looked, a corridor formed before her. There was no sun, or none that she could see. In fact, there was no real sky, just a ceiling of heavy golden mist. Ara had a sinking, dizzying feeling that above the mist the forest continued, that there was no up or down, just infinite branches of trees radiating outward from where they stood. Ara's heart began to beat wildly.

"*Welcome to the Treeways,*" announced Petal, who had flown to hover at her shoulder, as if sensing Ara's alarm.

Lysander floated several feet ahead, studying the trees and looking back at Ara every now and then.

"Few humans come here now. They don't know how to open the portals," Petal added.

Ara could feel her entire body vibrating with a new energy. She couldn't begin to describe it to herself mentally, so she gave up trying. Fighting back a wave of vertigo, Ara focused on the identical trees. "Is each one of these trees like a real tree, in our world?" she asked.

Lysander replied without turning back, and Ara noticed that his voice carried as if they were in water. *"Yes. At least, the ones that are mature enough. It is not quite your physical world, and not quite the spirit world, but both. And it is not an exact replica of their location in your world,"* he added.

Ara frowned. "So how do you know where you're going?" she asked.

"It helps most to have tree knowledge and to have drunk the sap of the tree you wish to visit. And some have markings if you know how to read them," Petal said quietly. *"But don't worry, we know where we're going!"*

Ara took tentative steps to the nearest tree, identical to all of the other tall straight giants, her feet sinking a few inches into the moss carpet with every step. She raised her right hand to the bark, its branches high above, somewhere in the mist. She paused for a few moments and closed her eyes to concentrate. It was warm; and the world to which it led felt light-filled and comforting.

"It's warm where this tree lives! There's sunlight," Ara said, her voice trailing off as she wondered how she could feel such a thing.

"The sun shines on the place of this tree, wherever it is in the world. Some are in darkness, or moonlight. Others are in snow and the bark is chilled," said Lysander.

Ara walked to the next tree, and then the next, sensing their warmth or light. "This one is warm, this one too," she announced as she made a little circuit.

Ara could feel the insects watch her intently as she returned to the portal tree. The opening had now dissolved back into a thick, nondescript bark and it appeared the same as the others. Ara shuddered at the prospect of being lost. "Let's go!" she announced.

"*There are many stops along the way,*" Petal said, and Ara felt her velvety wing brush against her cheek.

"*Yes, on to the first, to meet with the highest Elementals,*" agreed Lysander. He flashed his green light at Ara, as if to fortify her, and flew off in a clear direction between the endless rows.

Ara studied the trees as she followed behind, looking for hints of the Sleeping Ones. She occasionally brushed a hand against a trunk and received a buzz of electricity, or an image would flash in her mind of a place, or the sun, or lightning.

As the minutes wore on, Ara began to feel like they were being watched. She felt a presence behind her.

Ara spun around but glimpsed nothing except the uniform trunks. Frozen, she scanned the wood, the back of her neck tingling.

"*This way!*" Lysander called back.

Ara realized she was lagging and was just about to close the distance when a boy stepped from behind a nearby trunk. He was tall and solid, and seemed at home between the trees. He regarded Ara suspiciously before taking a step closer.

"What are you doing here? This stretch is usually empty," he said.

He kept glaring at Ara and she had time to notice that he wore roughly made leather clothes and sturdy lambskin boots. A bow was slung round his right shoulder and he carried a small bag filled with round things, maybe acorns. There was something wild about him, like he was used to sleeping outdoors.

"I'm going somewhere," she said in response, reluctant to share how happy she was to see another person in the Treeways until she learned more of who he was. "What are you doing here?"

The boy's face softened a fraction and he looked from Ara to the insects, who had now positioned themselves on her shoulders. A look of understanding entered his eyes.

"*He knows who we are—he will help you*," said Lysander at her ear.

Ara felt a flush of gratitude—they were perched as if on Tobias.

"Oh—I see you have friends. I come here to collect nuts and things," the boy explained, patting his bag. "Sometimes rabbits, but I make sure not to clean them here," he added.

"Well, why not?" asked Ara.

"You don't shed blood in the Treeways. That would be very bad luck; I thought you'd know that," he said, giving her a skeptical look yet again.

"Wait—we're speaking the same language. Where are you from?" he asked, folding his arms.

Ara thought she could tell him the truth. He seemed to know far more about the Treeways than she did, and he didn't look like a spy from the Citadel.

"I'm from Amethys, and I'm a student at the Citadel. Where are you from?" she asked, giving him an expectant look.

"Onea," said the boy, before looking away.

Ara had heard of Onea in history class. The place that Amethys had invaded years ago. "So you use the Treeways there? And you just come here for gathering nuts?" she asked.

The boy seemed to think this was obvious and gave a little shrug. "Or I use them to get to better hunting grounds. But I try to stick to the trees I know. One time I almost got lost in a snowstorm when I entered the wrong tree," he admitted.

"I don't know how you can tell the trees apart! If I didn't have the help of Petal and Lysander," Ara began, gesturing to the insects, "I would be in serious trouble."

Ara decided to step forward. "I'm Ara. I'm really happy to see another person here," she said.

The boy stepped closer. "I'm Heron," he said with a short nod.

"Which way are you walking?" Ara asked, hoping that he might walk with them for a bit.

Heron gestured in the direction they'd been traveling. "My home tree is up that way. I've found all I can carry for the day, anyway," he said, touching the bag. He resettled his bow and shifted his feet.

"Ok, maybe we can walk together for a bit?" Ara asked.

Without waiting for an answer, Petal and Lysander left Ara's shoulders and flew ahead.

"Sure," Heron replied and began to walk with Ara behind the insects.

Ara studied him carefully as they walked. His face looked kind now that he was no longer scowling. He had been so silent behind them, he had to be a very good hunter indeed. "Can I ask —how did you learn to enter the Treeways?"

Heron shot her a quick glance and Ara noticed that his eyes had softened. "Well, from my grandfather. He's a Treekeeper, and he usually opens them for me, or anyone from my village who is skilled enough to travel. But I can do it on my own now."

"Wow, your grandfather... I just learned recently from one of my teachers; he's a Treekeeper too, and a Shaman," she said.

Heron didn't seem surprised. "A bit odd for the Citadel, right?"

"Oh no, not at the Citadel... He lives in the forest," Ara explained.

Heron snorted and took a nut from his bag. "Those guys from the Citadel wouldn't know what to do if a tree fell in the woods," he added under his breath.

Ara had to agree with him, but stayed silent.

"Want a nut? They aren't too bad raw but I like them better roasted," he said, and pulled out a large round one.

Ara accepted it from his open palm and saw that he already had callouses on his hands.

"I've never seen this kind before," she said.

It was a rich brown color and smooth—it reminded her of a chestnut.

Ara watched Heron break his open easily and eat the flesh within. Ara tried to break hers open but couldn't manage it.

They walked in silence for a bit and then Heron said, "I'll open it if you want."

Ara handed it to him and muttered, "Thanks."

Heron had just handed it back to her when the ground beneath them shifted. The green carpet of moss crumpled in on itself, and for a fraction of a second, Ara's feet rested on air.

With a sickening drop in her stomach she plummeted beside Heron, whose hand almost grasped hers mid-air. They both fell with a thud into the waiting darkness. Ara heard Heron cry out as she bounced and rolled sideways into the newly formed pit.

Ara shifted in the soft mass of whatever she'd landed on. Everything felt dark and spongy, and she fought off the urge to sneeze. Her body ached a bit, but nothing seemed broken.

"Heron?!" she called into the darkness.

She heard a groan.

"Over here! Are you okay?" he asked.

"I think so! Where are we? What is this place?!" Ara called to him. He couldn't have rolled far.

"Keep talking!" he muttered, and Ara became aware of his approach across the spongy ground.

"Okay, I'm right over here. And now my eyes are adjusting. I'm sitting up," she announced, holding out her hands in front of her.

She patted his arm in the darkness and held on tightly. The Greenspell jumped to life on her arms and she whispered, "Settle!" without thinking. Thankfully, Heron didn't seemed to notice. Now she could see the look of awe on his face as he sat next to her.

"I've heard there were pockets of darkness in the Treeways, but I've never seen one. I think this must be one of them. Looks like another series of tunnels, or a nest," he remarked.

Ara tentatively got to her feet and peered up at the gaping hole in the moss several feet above them. Ara fought back a wave of fear. It was like a window to another world, maybe six feet across.

Petal and Lysander flitted around at the edge and stared down at them.

"*Are you all right?*" Petal called down.

"*We've never seen this before...*" Lysander said in a worried tone. "*It must be a lair.*"

"Thankfully, we haven't been hurt. But can you help us get out?" Ara called up.

Heron's eyes flashed quickly from the insects back to her. "What are they saying?" he asked.

Relieved that she didn't need to explain, she told him the truth. "He—the dragonfly is Lysander—thinks it's a lair of some kind. But I don't know if they have any ideas yet on how to get us out," she replied.

Heron stood up and began to walk around the space. "I need to find my bow," he muttered.

Now that her eyes had adjusted, Ara saw multiple tunnels fanning out from where she was sitting. There were dim lights in the tunnels that looked like candles carved into the walls. A phrase from her studies at the Citadel popped into her mind: "*As above, so below.*" It looked like a world of roots and darkness; a counterpoint to the Treeways but underground.

A vague shape was making its way towards them from the opposite direction, accompanied by faint shuffling noises.

"Heron!" she whispered. "Someone's coming!"

"Can you climb up? Are there roots down here?" Heron asked.

"Yes. But I'm not sure if I can reach them. Hold on."

Ara felt the ground squish beneath her feet. She knelt closer and gave it a sniff—it smelled like a fungus, or mold.

"I found it!" Heron whispered from the other side of the pit.

"And I see some roots—I have an idea!" Ara whispered back.

She held her hands out in front of her face as she walked deeper into the darkness, *squish, squish,* her feet sinking with every step. Her hands found the thin tendrils first. "Come alive!" she told the vines on her arms.

Ara felt the tingle and surge of energy through her hands as the Greenspell quickened and the leaves glowed faintly in the darkness. The shuffling noise had gotten louder behind them.

"I can't find my arrows! I don't know what you're doing, but I'll stand here," Heron said, stepping in front of her.

Without letting go of the roots, Ara saw the figure of a man approach down one of the tunnels. His walk was halting and slow, his head fixed at a creepy angle on a long and slender neck. Everything about him felt wrong.

Panic flooded her body and Ara grabbed the tendrils with new resolve. They might not be normal roots but they were connected to a living tree *somewhere.* She sent her mind as deep as it would go into the real tree that had made them, in the natural world. When she could feel the presence of the tree—it was resting, it was winter and she had woken it—she described where she was, and what she needed. Then the strange figure entered the space with them.

"Stop right there!" yelled Heron. He held his bow at shoulder height as if it had an arrow ready to let fly.

Ara gasped and froze, unsure of what was before her. It was reddish-brown, shaped like a man, and covered in layers of a rippling fungus. It had a large head and its eyes, nose and mouth were sliding down one side. Despite the tilt, the eyes were direct, glinting with malice and mockery. It chortled in response to Heron's cry, a deep, gurgling sound that made her stomach lurch.

"It's a rot ogre!" cried Petal, descending part way into the pit.

The rot ogre wagged its awful head and took a shaky step forward.

"Get back to your den!" cried Heron, drawing the bow.

Ignoring Heron, the rot ogre leered at Ara and the insects

who flew just out of his reach like small birds harrying a bird of prey. "Well, now... Look who's taken a tumble," came its hoarse voice, followed by hollow laughter. "I don't think your winged friends can help you down here. You're in my part of the Tree-ways now." The rot ogre gave them an oily grin.

So he could speak, after all, Ara thought. "Who are you? And what do you want?!" she cried.

"Why, what I always want. A little distraction, a little trea-sure. Visitors," he said.

And in the next moment, he caught Petal in one hand. Ara could almost feel the insect's shock and revulsion as she strug-gled against his spongy grip.

Ara dropped the feeble roots and felt the entire scene come into focus around her. She could see clearly the thick, puffy arm that held her friend and the challenge in his dark eyes.

Ara's heart flooded with power as she covered the distance between them in a second. She raised both hands and and imag-ined fire streaming from the Greenspell. She grabbed his arm and sank her fingers into the puffy flesh. She knew something was happening as his arm began to dissolve in her grip.

The rot ogre gave an awful scream and released his hold on Petal. Out of the corner of her eye, Ara saw her tumble to the ground and violently shake her wings. Lysander had flown down and landed beside her, his eyes locked onto the rot ogre.

Heron took the opportunity to jump behind the creature and pushed his bow into his back.

Ara saw frustration harden the rot ogre's gaze. Knowing she'd already done enough, she let go and felt the sweet relief of being free from his energy—it felt like decay and darkness beneath her hands.

"You'll be sorry for that," he said, clutching his arm. He wagged his head at Ara and took a few faltering steps away. Heron stayed behind him, until he'd reached the edge of the pit.

Ara could see his arm had already begun to reform itself. She hadn't meant to hurt him, just stop him, and so some part of her was relieved, regardless of how strange and awful he appeared to be.

"It will be nice to have you in my collection," he said as he turned back into a different tunnel from the one he'd come.

"Stay away!" Heron yelled at his retreating form, before turning to Ara. "You showed him! That was impressive. But we have to get out of here—now! He won't be gone long."

Ara's stomach churned and the fear she'd been holding at bay leapt again. "I know! I didn't know I could do that, but I'm glad it worked," she said, before checking on Petal. Her wings had dried, and she fluttered them slowly, as if testing them out.

"*We can fly out but you can't—continue working, Ara. We'll keep an eye on things from above,*" Petal said, before flying once more with Lysander to the top of the pit.

Relieved to see her uninjured, Ara walked back to the tiny tendrils of roots again—she'd just summoned fire, and it had worked, so maybe she could do more.

Taking a deep breath, she willed the Greenspell alive and sent a call to the tree, "*Roots thicker!*"

As the signal left her hands a few seconds passed in stillness. Ara felt Heron draw closer, but was grateful that he stayed silent.

At last, the tree answered her call. A surge of joy flooded her heart as the roots sprang to life beneath her fingers, growing thicker and firmer. Ara loosened her grip to let them wind and coil their way to the floor of the pit. She sent her thanks to the living tree, wherever it was in the world, and then grabbed another thin clump of roots to start again.

"What's on your wrists?" Heron whispered from her shoulder.

"It's called the Greenspell," Ara said. "I'm still getting used to it. It's a gift from a tree in the forest where I live." Maybe it would be best to be vague, Ara thought.

"So what powers does it give you then?" Heron asked, intent upon the glowing vines that snaked up her wrists and the growing roots in her hands.

"It feels like I know things through them. Like I know what plants are thinking, and even animals a bit. But I've only had it for a few days," Ara explained. She hoped that what she had just said made sense.

"That's like me with dreaming. Sometimes I see the future," Heron replied evenly. He seemed satisfied enough with her answer and turned away. "I'll go watch the tunnels," he whispered back.

Ara immersed herself in her task, moving from tree to tree, and soon had many sturdy ropes. With one ear focused behind her for the rot ogre, she stood back and considered the distance from the floor to the opening above. This time she sent an image to the trees, as a group. "*Now form a ladder!*" she told them.

At first the ropes just dangled where they were, unmoving. But after a few moments they began to creep closer in space as they lengthened toward one another. Ara gave a little jump as they wove themselves together before her eyes, creating a taut net for them to climb.

"Heron! Petal and Lysander—look!" she whispered.

"*Well done!*" Lysander said as he flew down to inspect the ladder. "*They answered your call.*"

Heron returned to Ara's side, and his eyes seemed to glow with a new-found respect. "I think this will work. Quick, get on and I'll follow you up," he said.

Heart thumping, Ara grasped the net and felt it sway forward as she placed a foot in a loophole. It softened beneath her and then flexed again in response to her weight. She reached for another loop and advanced a few inches farther. Ara climbed slowly and awkwardly at first as the net swayed and moved around her. But soon she got the hang of it and picked up speed, with the single focus of getting out. The net sagged again when Heron got on beneath her, but it didn't break.

When Ara had climbed about halfway she could see the light of the Treeways. She looked down at Heron's face in the darkness below and paused. The roots were sending her a message.

A blur of white racing down a tunnel flashed through her mind. Ara held the roots tightly and closed her eyes to focus. She mentally scanned the darkness below, searching... What had the rot ogre said about visitors?

Ara cast her mind deeper into the darkness until she felt something. There it was—it was at rest; it felt pure, and alone. Ara began to climb down.

"Ara, what are you doing?" asked Heron in a whisper from below.

"There's someone else here, someone trapped. I think we have to get them out!" Ara called down.

The heft of the ladder and the ease of the descent gave her more courage. She stopped where Heron was and gave him a level look. "I'm going to find whoever it is," she declared.

Heron huffed and reset his shoulders. "Are you sure?" he asked. Just like Nat would have asked.

Ara felt more sure of her decision once her feet met the spongy ground. "I'm sure," she replied. "There's something here that needs help—and now that we know how to get out, we at least have to look for it!"

"Okay...I'll come with you. But let's be fast, he might be back any time!" he said.

"*Ara*—" Petal began.

But Ara was already standing at the mouth of their chamber, carefully peering into the tunnels that fanned out around them. She counted six.

"The trees sent an image of someone trapped. We're going to go find them!" Ara said to the moth.

Petal gave Ara a serious look from her tiny onyx eyes. Ara didn't have the time to explain what she'd sensed.

She sent out a call through the Greenspell—"*We're here to get you! Where are you?*"—and hoped that it wouldn't be intercepted by the rot ogre.

Ara and Heron stood barely breathing at the edge of the pit. Ara felt her body being pulled by the third tunnel from the left.

It was darker inside, and it took a few seconds for her eyes to adjust. She placed a hand on the side of the tunnel wall to steady herself as Heron stepped forward.

"It's a trapped animal," he whispered to her. "I can feel it now."

Ara nodded. He took off down the tunnel and Ara followed close behind, grateful that they both knew how to walk in near silence.

As the tunnel curved to the right and down, Ara re-sent her message *"Where are you?"* A shiver of apprehension swept through her as she saw that the tunnel would soon branch into three.

Heron stopped for a moment to listen and then began to walk swiftly towards the middle tunnel. "This way!" he whispered, setting off at a jog.

Ara felt the hairs on the back of her neck begin to rise and the vines tingle on her arms as she propelled herself through the darkness behind him. It finally stopped at an abrupt angle. Ara placed her hands on the wall and peeked around the side with Heron.

Before them was a large round chamber with smooth walls interrupted only by a single tunnel at the far end. Piles of hay and sweet grass were strewn across the floor and a large bucket of water placed near the center. A wheelbarrow rested on its side near the tunnel opposite. In the center, tied to a stake in the floor, stood the most beautiful white horse Ara had ever seen.

A look of knowing shot through the horse's eyes and Ara's body trembled. She held her hands out before her and let a soft sigh escape her lips.

"She might be skittish—I don't mind being kicked. Let me see if she'll allow me to hold her rope," Heron whispered.

Ara watched as he reached out a hand to pat her nose ever so carefully. The mare shivered at his touch and closed her eyes.

"Untie her as fast you can!" whispered Heron, who now stroked her neck.

Ara jumped into action pulling apart the knots of the rough

rope wound about the stake. She felt sickened to touch this handiwork of the rot ogre that had kept this incredible creature trapped. Luckily, he had made easy knots and within moments, Ara held the loose end of the rope.

"Let's see if she'll come with us," Heron said as he looked into the animal's large black eyes.

"Ok, let's go slowly. We don't want her to get spooked and run down the wrong tunnel," added Ara. But Ara knew they didn't have much time before the rot ogre came back to check on them.

Heron nodded, and wrapped the rope around his wrist. The white mare pranced and tossed her head the moment they left her prison, the smell of freedom in her nostrils.

Ara walked beside her and stroked her neck in silence, calming her as best she could, while Heron tried to keep just the right pace—too fast and she'd break into a full run, too slow and she might bolt in the wrong direction.

Moments later they reached the next intersection and continued their climb up the first tunnel. Ara kept her ears and senses focused forward as she walked beside the mare, squeezing around her when the tunnel narrowed.

At the next turn, the air and light from the pit reached them. The mare's nostrils flared and as the open sky of the Treeways came into view, she pulled Heron forward. Ara watched Heron unwrap his wrist and let her run towards the rope.

As if they'd practiced the move a thousand times, Lysander and Petal suddenly appeared at her ears. The mare came to a full stop, listening to the unusual insects at either side of her head. And then she launched herself up the ladder in a dream-like blur, her hooves just caressing the net with the slightest touch as she took to the air.

Ara felt a surge of elation at the beauty of her escape. She was free! It had happened so fast, Ara barely had time to wonder how. And in the next moment she knew the rot ogre had returned—he was close now. She could hear him make his scraping, determined steps behind them.

"Hurry—get on!" Heron said in a full voice.

Ara grabbed her sack, lying on the ground where she'd fallen. And then she saw his quiver of arrows.

Heron seemed to read her mind. "Forget it, just get on the ladder!" he hissed.

Ara decided to obey and jumped on. Now that it was time to climb out for real her hands felt weak and shaky. She grabbed the net in both hands, and placed a foot as high as she could to gain some distance. The net swayed and rocked as she searched for purchase with her other foot, her back bowed out into the pit, exposed.

"You can't do that!" yelled the rot ogre.

Ara whipped her head around as he emerged from the intersecting space of the six tunnels. Heron had the arrow in one hand, and the net in the other.

The rot ogre was now only several feet away, his flabby arms outstretched. Ara had worried that Heron would linger to let her climb, but he jumped on the ladder and took the rungs two at a time. He had cleared the rot ogre's reach in seconds. Thank goodness he was slow on his feet, she thought, scrambling faster up the net. Ara focused on the glow of the Treeways above her. Lysander and Petal were gathered at the mouth of the pit, watching.

"You're almost there," Lysander called down in a calm, authoritative tone. *"I can see the moss ahead."*

Heron scrambled past Ara and made it to the top. He grabbed the upper part of the ladder and reached down to pull her up.

Ara had almost reached the top when the net swayed out from beneath her feet with the force of a new weight upon it. She let out a cry as she dangled from her arms and a soft hand closed around her ankle. Ara kicked her foot but the rot ogre pulled harder. She looked down. The rot ogre's eyes glinted with vengeance.

Like a streak of lightning, Ara sent an image through her hands to the trees and held on tighter. Before closing her eyes, she saw Petal descend from her perch on the moss.

"Hold on!" cried Heron, as he began to pull on her arms.

"Wait!" called the rot ogre from below, a note of panic entering his voice. "You don't have to do this! We can discuss whatever you'd like!" he continued on in a garble.

Ara felt his grip loosen on her ankle and kicked herself free. When she'd found her next foothold, Heron pulled her up onto the bed of moss at the lip of the sinkhole. Chest heaving, Ara exhaled with a shudder.

"Thank the light—that was close," said Heron.

He relaxed his grip on Ara's arms, and she turned her attention back down to the ladder.

Just as she'd envisioned, the ladder had rolled itself up into a loose ball, holding the rot ogre suspended off the ground, his arms and legs sticking out from its taut embrace. Petal approached his head where it protruded from the roots. He snarled as she drew close and fluttered something sparkling in his face with her wings.

The rot ogre sputtered and sneezed as he tried to reach her with one of his captive arms. Petal dodged his futile efforts and flew back to them. A few moments later the sounds of giggles wafted up from below. He sounded happy!

Ara turned to Petal in confusion. "What did you do?" she asked.

"*I gave him a little dust from my wings,*" Petal explained. "*He'll laugh himself to sleep, and he won't remember why he was so upset in the first place.*"

Ara studied the net for a few moments as the rot ogre's guffaws became softer. "Alright—shall I let him down, then?" she asked.

She didn't want to entrap him forever, that would be cruel.

But perhaps he might benefit from some experience of what he had inflicted on the mare. Ara shuddered at the thought there might be more creatures in the tunnels below.

"I don't know," Heron began.

"*If you must...*" Lysander said quietly.

In spite of his remark, Ara could tell they expected her to do just that. Ara crawled carefully to the edge of the pit, touched the very top of the root ladder and sent her message. Within moments the roots had almost completely released their hold on the rot ogre, and he was lowered gently down until he hovered just a foot off the ground. It didn't look like it would take him too long to get out. His odd mouth was flopped open, emitting gargles and what sounded like snores.

Satisfied, Ara got to her feet, backed away from the pit and made a short bow to her already-sleeping adversary. She held her forearms up in the muted light from above and studied the Greenspell. "Thank you," she whispered fiercely to this new magic.

Ara turned to Heron, but he was already making his way toward the mare with open hands. She'd walked off a fair distance and seemed hesitant at his approach but allowed him to take her lead.

Once they were back, Petal and Lysander hovered at each of her ears. The mare blinked a few times and looked from Heron to Ara. Ara could have sworn she said "thank you" through her eyes.

"How did she fly out of the pit?" Ara asked the insects.

"I was wondering that too—but I think this horse is special," Heron said. "That's why that thing had her trapped."

"This horse can fly in spirit—we were just reminding her," replied Petal.

Now that she was still and at rest, Ara could make out a faint blue sheen of light around her. So she was a magical horse—an Elemental, maybe, like the insects.

"I'll take care of her, I promise. I had a dream about it," Heron said with pride.

Petal and Lysander buzzed in approval and Ara relayed their message to Heron. He gave a shy smile and Ara knew he was telling the truth.

Ara and Heron walked the white mare a good distance from the open pit and didn't stop until they found an area that Petal and Lysander deemed safe. They agreed that they'd eat something and offer the white horse some food and water. Ara unwrapped the simple items she'd taken from Tobias's kitchen and offered what she had. Heron looked please with the bread and cheese, and the white horse daintily ate an apple.

"So—where are you going, for real?" asked Heron. He had now seen the power of the Greenspell, and his eyes were kind and curious.

"I'm going to the World Tree," she began.

Ara decided to tell him the main points of the story; they'd just been through a lot together and she trusted him. Ara described the Keeper's army and her quest for the Flaming Seed. Petal and Lysander had landed to listen and looked back and forth between Ara and Heron as she spoke. Ara felt like Lysander was about to speak to her privately, so she paused.

"*Tell Heron about the Sleeping Ones*," he whispered.

"Oh yeah—and I'm supposed to awaken some people or beings frozen in the trees here!" she added.

Heron had already finished eating and spent most of Ara's tale on his feet. He'd shot her a few keen glances when she mentioned the Citadel and the army. He now had his arm slung around the mare's gleaming white neck. This made Ara happy— the horse clearly liked him.

"Maybe I can help you. The World Tree is in Onea somewhere, I know that. My grandfather has spoken of it lots of times. But it's on sacred ground, hidden away somewhere behind a sea of mist. Or that's what it sounded like. As soon as I get back, I'll tell him all you've told me. He might have some ideas on how to keep that army away," he said, scowling.

Ara's heart leapt at this news.

Heron pointed deeper into the Treeways. "And I've seen what you're talking about—people in the trees. There are some over there, and a few near my home tree," he said.

"Really? Can you show me?" Ara asked.

"Yeah—I can do that before I bring her home with me," he replied.

Heron led the way through the Treeways, the white mare at his side. At last he drew close to one particular tree. It was thicker than the ones around it and Ara could see the outline of a woman's face beneath the bark. There was an elbow too, and a knee. She held something in her hand, and she was curled up, as if resting. Ara could only see her face in profile. Was she sad? Or was that her natural sleeping expression?

"Do you know what to do?" Heron asked beside her.

Ara shot him a quick look. "No! But I'm going to try waking her up with the Greenspell. I guess we'll see what happens," she replied.

Ara held out her hands, and whispered, "Come alive!" The green tendrils stirred and wound across her wrists, eliciting a gasp from Heron.

Ara suddenly knew what to do. *The tree must have a seal on it*, she thought, *like the portal trees*. But this seal kept the being trapped within it. Maybe Ara could remove it or override it with the Greenspell.

Taking a deep breath, Ara placed both hands on the trunk.

Thump-thump. Thump-thump.

The tree had a heartbeat.

Ara's mind went blank for a moment as she realized it belonged to the sleeping woman.

Eyes screwed shut with concentration, Ara spoke to the Greenspell and the tree at once. *"Reveal!"*

Ara felt a strange sizzling and opened her eyes a crack. Light began to issue from around her fingertips, and a black symbol became visible on the bark. "*Clear!*" she sent, keeping her eyes open.

The black symbol began to melt as the golden symbol—a spiral—grew stronger and brighter on the bark. Now the Greenspell surged and the leaves grew brighter. Ara's hands began to grow hot but she was afraid to move them.

"Look! She just blinked an eye!" cried Heron, who'd walked closer to the tree.

Afraid to break her concentration, Ara closed her eyes again. The bark was now soft and malleable beneath her hands. In just another moment it would be like water.

Ara heard someone gasp for breath, like they'd been underwater far too long. Something moved powerfully from the tree and Ara jumped back, hands still in the air before her.

The woman now sat on the ground, gasping like a fish. She looked from Ara and Heron to the tree, and back. The Greenspell had settled but Ara could still almost feel the woman's heartbeat, loud and strong in the air around her.

In one swift motion, the woman bowed deeply to Ara and then stood. She was tall and slender, and dressed in many shades of green. A long flow of silver hair fell down her back, from which sprouted a set of clear wings, lined in gold. She had a bow, and a small dagger clutched in her right hand.

"Whoa," Heron said.

Ara still couldn't speak. Petal and Lysander flew to hover at her face. She watched a quick telepathic exchange pass between the woman and the insects.

The woman turned to Ara and gave her a long, warm gaze. For a moment, Ara could almost hear her voice. And then she spoke.

The woman's voice was beautiful and strong, as if she'd just been singing and not frozen near death in a tree. Ara and Heron exchanged quick glances as the syllables of her unknown words washed over them like a blessing.

Ara looked to Lysander, who'd landed upon her shoulder. The woman stopped speaking and bowed once more.

Lysander translated: "*She says—thank you for freeing me, little sister. She's been trapped here for perhaps thousands of years, since one of the last wars with the forces of darkness. She did not expect one so young to find her. She has other kin stuck in the trees. If you will permit her, she will show you, and then lead you on the next phase of your journey.*"

"What is she?" Ara asked him.

"*Isn't it clear? She is winged. She is both human and Elemental. She is from an age long past,*" he replied.

"And I'm her sister?!" Ara pressed.

"*Yes, in a way, in the old green lineage,*" said the dragonfly.

Ara wanted to ask more but the woman was clearly waiting. Ara stepped closer and bowed to her. "I'm Ara! And yes, I'll free them if I can," she said.

The woman nodded and said, "Silwa."

Heron introduced himself to her with an awkward bow and the woman made a motion for drinking. Heron quickly produced a waterskin and offered it to her. While Silwa drank in large gulps, Ara and Heron studied her closely.

"I can't believe she has wings! Can she actually fly?" Heron asked.

Silwa had just finished drinking and beat her wings very slowly, as if testing them out. The look on her face was one of sorrow.

"Lysander—can she still fly, after all this time?" Ara asked the dragonfly.

Lysander approached Silwa and gently landed on her forearm. She smiled and Ara knew they were communicating. She shook her head and spoke aloud to him.

"*She says she cannot fly in this air—it's different than the air she remembers. It feels too heavy,*" Lysander reported back to Ara.

Heron shook his head after hearing Ara's explanation. "Maybe she'll be able to fly again someday. She must be ancient... that's the only thing that makes sense. I've never heard that language before. Look! There's more of them over here," he said, pointing to some trees nearby.

Silwa finished drinking and led Heron and Ara to one of the other trees. She touched the tree wistfully. Lysander landed on her hand.

"*It's her brother; his name is Somae,*" he announced.

Ara steeled herself for another round of magic. This time the being that emerged came out standing. Powerfully muscled and dressed in black, his wings were edged in gold like Silwa's. He looked around for several moments in a daze. Ara wasn't sure if he even noticed her kneeling beside the base of the tree.

Once his eyes refocused, Somae took both of Ara's hands in his own and bowed to her deeply in thanks. And then he saw his sister and lifted her off the ground in a bear hug. Both Ara and Heron had to look away as they enjoyed a reunion filled with many gasps and tears.

Ara called Lysander and Petal over for translation. "How did they feel in the trees? And what do they think now?" she asked.

Lysander hovered between Ara and Heron's faces, creating a little triangle. "*They aren't sure yet how much time has passed. It sounds like they were fully asleep in the trees, maybe dreaming. They don't remember many details of their sleep—just the moments leading up to their imprisonment,*" he said.

"And what happened?" Heron asked, after Ara had translated.

Petal floated down to rest on Heron's forearm, and Ara saw his face light up. "*It sounds like they were in the midst of traveling from one place to another during a battle, and some entity sealed them off entirely,*" she said.

Close to an hour later, Ara had freed four more human Elementals. Each one resembled Silwa in one way or another, but they all had different faces and skin tones representative of the entire human family. There was Larch, a willowy man dressed in green and gray, a woman with large pink wings named Haru, and a woman with blue-tipped wings and cat-like eyes named Sowelo.

Ara sat exhausted on the ground after the last one was

freed—a large man with a dark beard and silver-etched wings named Ogran. Between the six of them they carried enough supplies for making camp, as Ara noted a small cauldron on the back of Sowelo and tents and mats on the backs of Larch and Ogran.

Heron joined Ara on the moss and they watched the group cry, hug and laugh. "Can you imagine being trapped in a tree that whole time?" he whispered. Ara shook her head. "Now that you have them with you, I think I need to go back and warn everyone."

Ara looked up into Heron's eyes and felt a short pang at seeing him leave. It felt like they were friends now. "I understand. You need to get home," she said.

But before he left, there was something she needed to know. "Heron—could you find the portal tree I came through to get here, if you had to? And can you show me yours?"

"Yes. They both have a Shaman's markings. Your tree is back that way," he said, gesturing in the direction they'd come. "And mine's over here," he answered.

Heron got to his feet and grabbed the white mare's reins that lay on the ground nearby. She hadn't left his side the entire time, and Ara could tell that they were meant to be together.

Heron led Ara to a nearby tree and pointed at some squiggly lines on the bark that could have been carved, or grown there naturally, it was hard to tell. "See these lines? That tells you it's a portal tree. Now you'll know what to look for."

Ara let her fingers flutter across the wavy lines. "Okay—thanks! I'll remember."

Heron gave a short nod and then began to walk back to Silwa and the group.

Ara followed alongside, one hand on the mare's neck. Heron said a short goodbye to Silwa and her kin before he circled back to her. Ara took a step forward, not exactly sure what she was about to do.

Heron dropped the reins, grasped her hands in his and held

them up to his chest. "Good luck, Ara," he said. "I'm glad I met you... Be in the light."

"Thank you, Heron. You, too..." she trailed off, as she joined her other hand to his.

Ara felt something run through her hands and up her arms as the Greenspell awakened. A small, quiet certainty grew in her being—she would see him again.

Heron cleared his throat and released her hands. Ara watched him pick up the reins once more and walk with the white mare towards his home tree.

Ara followed the two figures until they stopped at the one particular tree he'd shown her, that looked like all the others save for the markings. Heron did something Ara couldn't see, and in the next moment boy and horse had passed through.

$$\text{\foreignlanguage{}{❦}} \quad 8 \quad \text{❦}$$

"*She is asking—are you ready?*" said Lysander at her ear.

Ara turned to see Silwa and the dragonfly right behind her. Silwa gave her a warm look that said she understood these sorts of goodbyes.

"I'm ready," she replied, knowing that it was only partly true.

"*We each thank you, little sister—for returning us to life. We have much to learn and seek the heads of the Elementals now,*" Lysander said. "*They will renew us and show us what we need to know. Tell us how you came to be here, and what is your journey?*"

Silwa had stopped speaking and she had an expectant look on her face. Ara gazed quickly at the six sets of eyes—ancient, wise and yet curious. She thought they were almost child-like. "I think you have been sleeping for a long time," she began.

Ara described current-day Amethys, the Citadel, the Keeper, Tobias, and her search for the Flaming Seed at the World Tree. As her tale wore on, she noticed the looks of shock, sorrow and resolve. Ara wondered if there were any human Elementals left on Earth—perhaps they were the last.

They talked amongst themselves for several minutes, and Ara watched each one of their faces. At different times one would gesture and Ara would see a flash of light over their heads in gold or red. Trying not to be too nosey, Ara wandered off a bit further into the Treeways but was careful to not go too far—she didn't want to fall into a pit!

Petal landed on her shoulder at last, and Ara took comfort in the soft violet wing that beat against her cheek.

"The six have come to a decision, I think," she said, leading Ara back to the group.

Silwa stepped forward and spoke while Lysander translated at Ara's ear. Silwa gestured to her kin and then to Ara and deeper into the Treeways.

"She says that they will journey to the World Tree with you and help you find the Flaming Seed. They must ready themselves to fight this new enemy and are eager to leave this place of their entrapment."

"Okay—that sounds good. Thank them for me—I'm so grateful to have help. The Guardian of the Flame said I would, and this is so much better than I thought!" Ara replied aloud.

She let Lysander communicate with the six and took in their fond glances and warm nods of acknowledgement. And with that, they set off through the Treeways once more.

Ara walked between Silwa and her brother Somae in the front, happy to have their guidance. Now she had a better chance to study their wings, each one with intricate tracings of lines and shapes like a clear butterfly wing. Ara watched their feet roll across the emerald moss and realized that they barely left a footprint, while her boots made deep indents with every step.

Silwa and Somae chatted quietly amongst themselves, largely ignoring Ara until they came to a stop before an unusual black tree. It stood identical in size, but unlike the others its bark was black and smooth as polished onyx. Silwa reached out a hand and drew a symbol on the trunk. Almost immediately the bark began to swirl, and a green door covered in silver writing took its place. Silwa pushed on the door and it swung in effortlessly. She shot a smiling glance back to Haru and Ogran bringing up the rear and motioned for Ara to step through.

Ara entered a grove of giant redwood trees. It was nearing dusk, and the sky was a rich violet dappled with early evening stars. Tiny pinpricks of light sparkled up and down the trees and circled in the air all around. Ara realized they were fireflies of many different colors, dancing amidst the trees. Large bats, their faces like fuzzy golden foxes, swooped in between them, making the fireflies flash anew.

Silwa stood beside her, a great smile on her face. She sang out a wild whoop and Ara heard a buzzing in the air, and something that sounded like music.

Once they were all through the portal, Ara watched Sowelo seal the tree. She turned back to the glowing, magical scene before them, let out a piercing cry of joy and kissed the ground.

"*We are in a rare place that few humans visit—a true temple of nature,*" explained Petal from the air at Ara's shoulder.

Ara saw twelve enormous redwoods aligned like great columns just ahead, and an open space between them. Silwa walked over and took Ara's hand, as she stood looking around in a daze. As more lights jumped to life around them, tiny prisms gathered at her eyelashes. A fragrance of flowers and herbs wafted through the air, strong enough for her to taste.

Ara let Silwa lead her to the twelve trees, where most of the group were already waiting. With every step, Ara felt lighter, and stronger. She had a sense that she'd been here before but couldn't explain why.

Silwa paused between two of the giant redwoods and bowed deeply, both hands over her heart. She stepped between them into the invisible temple and looked back at Ara with a faint smile.

Ara paused for a moment to look up to the tops of the trees, spangled with tiny lights. She repeated Silwa's gestures and entered between the redwoods.

Something fluttered down from above and a luna moth landed on one of Ara's forearms. It flapped its feathery silver green wings a few times, each one with a perfect round dot and a beautiful pattern of shading along its edges.

"*Welcome!*" said a chime-like voice in Ara's mind.

Ara smiled in delight and answered the moth, *"Hello! Thank you!"* before it flew away.

Silwa then drew Ara to the open space where the others were already assembled on stone seats around a large black log, their faces reverent. Ara stood a bit off to the side as one by one they placed a hand on the log and closed their eyes.

A soft gust of wind whirled around them, lifting the hair at the back of Ara's neck. Somae began to sing in a near whisper, and then he was joined by Silwa and the others with each new verse. The words sounded primordial, like the sounds of waves on surf, or tree branches alive in the wind; sounds to call forth the heads of the Elementals.

The blackened log began to glow with shimmering lights, as waves of violet, green, blue, and gold rippled across the surface from somewhere deep within. Ara looked on in wonder as the lights became both sound and light. Colors danced across the log and an otherworldly music issued from within. Ara leaned in closer to hear it ripple in waves on the air, rhythmic and lush. Something began to swell in her ears as the music whirled around her and through her in ribbons of air. Ara thought she heard her own name and felt her ears pop as the music stretched to the edges of the rows of redwoods, the walls of the invisible temple and up into the starry sky.

Sowelo came first to the log and Ara watched her beat her wings in the sound and light. She laughed aloud when the rhythm was fast enough for her liking, and then another of the kin took her place, as each one renewed their wings.

Gradually, four long columns of light appeared in four corners of the temple. They reached as far as the eye could see, up, up into the sky—blue, silver-white, green-gold, and the brilliant orange of sunset. The six dropped their hands and bowed their heads to the illumined newcomers.

Ara could barely breathe as an elaborate conversation took place between the small band of humans and the great columns of light. There was much nodding and Ara thought it looked like the humans were listening intently to each beam as it shared its information or wisdom that only the six could hear.

At last the columns faded into darkness and the log went still. Most of the group left the log and walked off into the forest.

Now it was fully dark, and as Ara turned to Silwa, still sitting on the ground, she could just make out her expression. "What were those columns of light?" Ara whispered, before realizing that neither Lysander or Petal were nearby to translate and tried to find their lights amidst all of the fireflies.

"They are the water, earth, fire and air in their light forms," she replied with a smile.

"Air has given us back our wings, and you too have been given knowledge, no?" Silwa said warmly.

Ara turned to her slowly, a look of awe on her face. "I—I understand you now!" she said in a near whisper.

"Yes, I believe you do," Silwa said with a laugh.

"But—" Ara began.

"It's part of their magic—don't think about it or it might stop working!" she advised.

Ara decided to trust her, and they walked to join the others at camp. She gladly took Silwa's hand as they began to walk from the invisible temple. Ara saw an inviting campfire and a group of well-made tents just past the redwoods. Haru stood over the fire stirring a pot while Larch sat on the ground, weaving something from grass. Ara looked longingly at the tents, suddenly feeling a wave of fatigue.

"It's time to celebrate!" Silwa sang out.

To help herself stay awake, Ara took turns stirring the pot that smelled of stewed apples, she collected fallen branches for kindling and helped to weave sleeping mats.

The moon had risen by the time they all sat around the fire

for a savory dinner of dandelion greens, stewed fruits and some sort of tuber Ara had never seen before. In between bites she'd asked Silwa what it was, but she didn't have a clear name for it— something like "ground plums". She'd also asked where on Earth they were, exactly, but was told that there was no name for it— the location didn't exist on human maps.

When the moon was high overhead, Larch played music on an instrument he'd woven from grass. Ara had found its sound strange at first but soon had trouble keeping her eyes open by the fire. Haru led her to one of the tents, sealed tight and cozy, smelling of fresh leaves.

In her last moments awake, Ara could see through the opening of the tent. The forest was a kaleidoscope of blinking lights, as thousands of fireflies flew from branch to branch. She saw the glowing eyes of animals just beyond reach of the fire, observing peacefully from a distance.

Was she really here, in an unknown place of magic? Ara placed a palm flat on the ground for reassurance. What came to her felt like a faint hum, or vibration. Maybe it was the sound of the Earth singing. Whatever it was, it soothed her, and within moments she was asleep.

The Keeper waited for his eyes to adjust to the darkness before speaking. He stood to his full height, his head just brushing the ceiling of the cell deep below the Citadel. A barely perceptible light filtered down with a thin trickle of fresh air from many feet above.

Now he could make out the figure of a large bird at the center of the room. It stood completely still and nearly resembled a child in a cloak save for its taloned feet. The Keeper hadn't bothered to chain its ankle—there were no windows through which it could fly and a sturdy metal lock on the door. The bird had access to water and food at a small table, but it appeared untouched. His old friend was surrounded by a thin layer of golden light, the Keeper saw. He had to be up to something.

The Keeper cleared his throat. He took another step forward and golden eyes jumped out of the darkness. Their power caught him off guard for a split second, but he soon recovered, and spoke: "For the first time in quite a long time, I can say that I am very happy to see you."

The Keeper watched as a flicker of fear appeared in the golden eyes and the bird flapped his wings. "But what is your aim, Tobias? You have already failed at everything else... Did you hope to usurp me by coming here? Or did you have the arrogance to think you might heal me?" he asked, suppressing the urge to chuckle along with the Dark Spirit.

The golden eyes narrowed a fraction. "*My presence is meaningless and you know it... Your time has come to a close, Grolyn. Can you not read the messages from the higher realms?*" Tobias's voice flowed unimpeded in the Keeper's mind, like rushing water. The Voice skittered to the side and the Keeper exhaled loudly. He was about to get angry.

"They are useless! And they abandoned us long ago, my friend. Have you been sleeping in the forest this entire time? Have you not felt the advance of our power—real power—in this very realm? Or mystic that you are, have you forgotten the physical?"

The golden eyes closed for a few seconds and then reopened. Now his voice was a roar. "*Have you forgotten everything, Grolyn? How much has this thing destroyed your mind? You are the one who closed off the connection to nature, the stars, and the light, not the other way round!*"

The Keeper experienced a split second of doubt—What had he forgotten?—before pushing it aside. He wouldn't let Tobias speak in his mind again. He could feel that his old friend's power and mastery outstripped his own. He now understood who the girl was, and how she could be of use. The Dark Spirit had shown him all.

"First I will take your memories of the girl—" he said. The Dark Spirit's voice almost spoke through him now, panting in his ear.

The Keeper watched as the hawk tried to mount a defense. He waited a few moments more until he had woven a lattice of light around his head. It was impressive, but not nearly strong enough.

The Keeper lowered the walls of his mind and let the Dark Spirit come through, unfettered. Since regaining his strength, he had tamed it well. They had a truce, so to speak. He forged a funnel between his mind and the delicate lattice hanging before him. Letting the Dark Spirit run free was like letting a pack of starving wolves loose on their long-sought prey.

The golden eyes closed with a shock as the Keeper invaded his memories with formidable strength. He stood like a shadow beside Tobias as Ara entered the black elm for the first time and stumbled inside, and much later when she climbed the tree at the approach of the hunters. The Keeper watched as Tobias left with the huntsmen, leaving Ara alone in the branches.

In this joined state, both Tobias and the Keeper could feel what happened next. A flood of gratitude swept through Tobias and an equal wave of frustration through the Keeper. She was no longer in the Great Boreal Forest. She had entered the Treeways —a place unknown to the Keeper. But now he knew her aim was the World Tree.

A slow dawning came upon the Keeper as the Dark Spirit scoured Tobias's mind to retrieve every image. There was more here, buried in his memory. Something important that the Keeper had forgotten. He tucked the knowledge away for safe-keeping and pulled the Dark Spirit back.

"Now, how do I pierce the mist? You are a master of the elements, if I remember correctly. Yes, you were proud of that, weren't you? The World Tree is just beyond that heavy veil. I have reports of its dimensions—far larger than even I imagined. My army stands before it on a plain in Onea. You know the words to say—tell me," instructed the Keeper, as if nothing had happened.

"*It is not so simple, Grolyn. You can't invade—your army will be stranded in the gray mist indefinitely. The Tree will protect itself and seal you there, no matter what you command of air or water. Your vibration is too low, and you reek of the misuse of power,*" Tobias said.

"Nonsense! There has to be a way. You and I know it—" said the Keeper before it dawned on him: the Dark Spirit was right—the girl was a key. What he needed was a human beyond the veil that could act as a homing device. He could focus all of his forces there, and pierce through.

She was still alive, he could tell. And she would make it to the World Tree.

Already his thoughts were on their next steps, and he could feel his mind being pulled away from the hawk, who flapped his wings in frustration. It was time to set things in motion.

❦   *9*   ❦

"HELLO, ARA! SILWA ASKED ME TO AWAKEN YOU..." SOWELO said, holding out a small warm cup.

Ara blinked her eyes open to see Sowelo's face close to hers, her large eyes bright in the darkness of the tent. Still groggy, Ara took the cup and muttered "thanks" as she sat up. Sowelo explained that they were all getting ready to leave and packing up camp. Ara noticed that she already wore a bag around her shoulder.

"We fly to the World Tree today," she said, before exiting Ara's tent.

Ara finished the warm water with herbs, gathered her things and stepped out into the early morning light. Ogran and Somae were busy taking down the other tents and Haru appeared to be gathering leaves with Larch a bit farther into the trees.

Ara stretched and looked around for Petal and Lysander. She didn't see them right away and then called to them softly in the branches above. Ara's heart leapt to see the moth and dragonfly loop down from one of the trees close by. She'd been so tired the night before she'd forgotten to say goodnight to them.

"*Did you sleep well, Ara?*" asked Petal sweetly as she landed on

Ara's shoulder. Ara enjoyed the brush of her wings against her cheek.

"I did! I was so tired that I fell asleep right away," she admitted. "What did you two do?"

"Lysander stayed up late with the fireflies—they had a symphony of lights! And I slept over your tent," she said.

"Thanks, Petal," she replied as Silwa approached from between the trees. She looked at Ara's sleepy face and then to the horizon.

"We must travel quickly today if we're to make it to the World Tree in time. We have a short stop to make first—there is a sleeping fire dragon that we will ask for a favor. If all goes well, we will be at the World Tree by day's end," she announced.

Ara's eyes widened at her words. "You mean—a real dragon? And he or she will come with us?" she asked.

"That is our hope. We are nearly ready to walk there," she said, before turning away to other tasks.

Ara stood idly for a few moments and then made her way to what was left of the campfire. Sowelo had already packed her cooling cauldron away but had left the ground plums wrapped in oak leaves nearby. Ara helped herself, taking a few bites of one and then adding the rest to her bag. She helped Larch pack the woven mats and sweep the ground for anything they'd left behind. Minutes later, the group set off through the forest away from the invisible temple, Petal and Lysander darting between them.

Ara tried to ask as many questions as she could of whomever would talk to her. She found that Haru had the most to say about their lives before, as she readily described what their world was like. It sounded like one of magic and myth—there were massive animals, cities in caves, libraries in the forest, complex methods of navigation. Ara couldn't piece it all together, but she enjoyed hearing Haru talk about her healing work with animals. It almost reminded her of her grandmother.

Larch told Ara about his skills with plants—how he could

speak to them and help them grow, and how he made his own music with whatever he had on hand. Sowelo explained how she made food and medicines in their old world—and how she could decipher snowflakes and lightning. Ogran showed her a crystal he used to read the rays of the sun and asked her many questions as well.

Ara had to hurry to chat with Somae, who walked briskly with his sister at the front. He seemed rather quiet and busy and so Ara only got a few words out of him. He'd been trained as a warrior. He'd fought in many battles with an unnamed foe. He tried to say vigilant for lions and wild boar.

The dense redwood forest gradually shifted to cedar, and the cedar gave way to green hills and open grasslands. They followed a winding brook with gleaming white stones through the grass, while in the distance, Ara could see a series of deep purple canyons etched into the earth.

The sun was almost overhead by the time Somae and Silwa finally stopped walking. They stood before the mouth of one of the purple canyons, a look of intensity on their faces. The canyons were tall and narrow, like someone had dragged a comb through molten rock. Shielding her eyes from the sun, Ara peered up at the purple walls and the sparse, spindly vines that clutched at their sides. Petal and Lysander flew to Silwa as the group paused in silence.

Ara watched the six share a brief telepathic exchange and make a decision. Silwa approached Ara and placed a hand on her shoulder.

"Just follow what we do—first we must ask permission to enter, and then we need to awaken him gently," she said.

The anxiety must have begun to show on Ara's face because Silwa continued—"And do your best to show no fear!"

Ara swallowed and nodded in what she hoped was a convincing way. They were going to awaken a sleeping dragon and she was supposed to stay calm and collected? An image of

Ember standing beside her saying, "*Steady, steady!*" in a jesting way popped into her mind, and helped her calm down.

Silwa and Somae bowed deeply at the mouth of one of the avenues. They waited in silence for the answer to their request for permission and entered when it had been given. Ogran and Sowelo went next, followed by Larch and Haru.

At last Ara bowed, hoping permission was granted for her as well and looked down at the purple sand beneath her feet with thanks. Larch shot her a kind look and Lysander returned to hover at her shoulder.

Ara tried to walk as quietly as possible so as not to disturb the sleeping dragon. Gone were what Ara thought of as green sounds of activity—birds, the chirping of insects—replaced by an eerie hush. Ara looked down at her walking boots and felt the soft shush of the pebbly sand beneath them as she kicked up little clouds of purple dust. A strong gust of wind rushed down the canyon to push at their faces and made a faint whistle as it passed through, melodic and strange.

As the canyon turned, the green fields disappeared from view behind them. Ara stifled a cough and focused on Silwa and Somae, several feet ahead, alert and on guard. The canyon walls narrowed around them, almost translucent in places, reminding Ara of Tobias's amethyst fireplace.

She reached out her fingertips as she drew alongside the wall. Smooth and warm, the stone seemed to zing with life, awakening the leaves of the Greenspell on her arm. Bewildered, Ara quickly drew her hand away before anyone noticed.

Long, white markings appeared on the walls as they rounded another bend. Ara veered closer to study one that ran along the ground. Was it a message? A chill swept through her as she realized they weren't symbols—they were bones.

As they rounded the next corner, Haru began to hum, like the drone of bees in a hive. Soon everyone else joined in and Ara mimicked their sound, feeling her body run hot. She did her best to stifle the urge to run ahead, away from the constraining purple walls.

The ground beneath them rose gently, and as the canyon wound yet again, the end came into view. At the very edge of the canyon a huge dragon lay sleeping, iridescent purple like the canyon walls. Curled up like a cat, it obstructed the last stretch of canyon before fields of green.

Ara stopped. The dragon had already opened one eye, and it was just opening the other. Two massive pupils looked back at them, large as doorways. It blinked a few times, as if still focusing its eyes, and then it sat up on its front legs, as high as a house. It looked at the small group of humans standing in the path and unleashed a torrent of purple fire into the sky. Ara dropped to the ground, shielding herself with her arms as she looked up at the underside of its jaw.

Before the dragon had finished its roar, Silwa floated several feet off the ground. And then each member of the group joined her, making a semi-circle in front of the dragon's face. It met their eyes as it lowered its head, and all six broke into song. Ara could nearly see its surprise as the wall of sound washed against its massive snout. It closed its eyes for a moment, as if enjoying the sensation. Once the dragon was mollified, the six floated down to earth once more.

Fully awake, the dragon shook its head and stretched its legs and spine. Now it looked around the canyon with a peaceful, curious expression.

Ara slowly sat up from her cowering position on the ground. She watched in awe as Haru drew closer and held out a hand for the dragon to sniff, as if greeting a strange dog. The dragon took her scent, grunted, and blew out a blast of air from his nostrils. Haru bowed respectfully, and then stepped away for another to take her place.

At last it was Ara's turn and Silwa waved her forward. "It's alright—he won't harm you now. Just introduce yourself," she said.

Ara stood up slowly, feeling all eyes upon her. The air seemed to crackle and buzz around her as she began to walk forward. Her mind slowed to a crawl as she drew closer, taking in its enormous size, the great black eyes that looked down at her from within a face that defied description. It was reptilian, yet reminded her of a giant dog.

She drew near, and finally stopped at the dragon's claws. She held out a hand and saw the Greenspell zing to life on its own as her hand traveled through the air as if unattached to her body. It paused in the warm space beneath the dragon's nostrils.

The dragon closed his eyes for a few seconds as he breathed in the Greenspell, and whatever information came from her small hand. He tilted his head to the side, as if considering something, and then let out a satisfied grunt. Ara felt her body relax as he turned his great eyes down towards hers with something like fondness.

"Now why don't you ask him if he'll let you ride him?" announced Silwa.

Ara flipped around to look at her, and then looked for Petal and Lysander, whom she now considered her friends and steady guides. "You mean—I'm supposed to ride him?! That's how we're getting to the World Tree?" she exclaimed.

"That's how you'll get there. We can fly now at will; air saw to that," she replied, with a quick glance at the other five kin, still standing in a semi-circle before the dragon.

"You can talk to him easily, you'll see. Place your hand on his claw. I'll stay here with you," sent Lysander at her ear.

But how was she supposed to ride him, Ara wondered, as she looked over the massive purple body of the dragon. His wings were still obscured behind its back.

She thought he looked docile enough to get closer and did as Lysander suggested. She reached down and touched the dragon's talons. *"Hello, I'm Ara. I'd be very grateful if you would let me ride on your back to the World Tree!"* she sent.

Ara felt the dragon's life force now, ancient and vast beneath her hands. He was a magical being of great power, a fire spirit able to shape the land in many worlds. He slept and awoke in cycles, and he had been sleeping for a very long time. His nature was gentle, but sometimes he enjoyed feasting in his dragon form. He breathed out and a warm stream of air rippled across her legs and stirred the Greenspell on her arms. And then Ara heard his voice in her mind, warm and deep.

"I remember these other humans with you—but not your kind of human. You are an unusual human without wings. Show me who you are," he said.

As he spoke, Ara became aware of his heart beat, like a great bass drum that echoed through his chest. It seemed to beat only once in a while, while hers beat nonstop. Ara sent as many images of herself as she could, forming a cascade of information of her short life, from her home with her family, to the Citadel, and how she'd come to stand before him now.

"I see..." said the dragon, who closed his eyes.

Ara had the sense that he understood her on a deep level, far beyond what she could ever show.

Ara waited, as the dragon sat in perfect stillness. She felt the seconds drag by, but she was too afraid to sever their connection. *"Climb on my head—and hold on tight while I test my wings."*

Ara looked up into the dragon's face, and then to Silwa and the group, who were clearly awaiting an answer. With a surge of confidence, she approached the dragon's neck, grasped one of his long, purple horns and climbed on, finding just the right spot at the back of his neck to perch. His skin was thick, and she somehow found places for her feet. The dragon sat up straight and stretched his enormous wings.

Somae let out a whooping call and the rest of the band broke into applause. Ara grinned down at them and let herself laugh aloud. She was on a dragon!

The dragon shifted around and was kind enough to ask Ara if she felt secure where she was. When she answered "no", he had her climb down and set about creating a saddle.

After several minutes of trial and error, Somae and Ogran had fashioned a saddle near the base of the dragon's neck from a combination of leather skins and cords they had between them. It was decided that Lysander and Petal would ride in Ara's bag, since they wouldn't be able to fly as high and fast as a full-grown dragon, but the human Elementals were ready for flight.

"We will travel in a circle, around you, to make sure all is well. Best put this on," Silwa said, and handed Ara up a blanket that one of the band had stored amongst their travel gear. "It gets chilly up there," she added.

Grateful, Ara slipped it around her shoulders. "How long until we get to the World Tree?" she asked, resettling herself in the saddle.

"Perhaps an hour or more... We'll see," she replied.

Ara watched Somae and Haru crouch down in a lunge. With a laugh, Ogran joined, and then Sowelo and finally Silwa took the position. Silwa yelled out an eerie cry and all six launched themselves into the air.

Ara watched in wonder as they cycled their legs a few times to gain height, and then their wings took over, each set beating rapidly. The joy on their faces was unmistakable. They drifted higher, and higher, and Ara thought that they were getting too far ahead.

"*Now hold on tighter than you ever have,*" said the dragon.

Ara steadied herself and grasped a spiny place on his neck. The dragon extended his wings and lowered into a deep crouch. She swallowed and closed her eyes.

Ara's stomach seemed to hit the ground as the dragon launched himself into the air. Ara felt the great beating of his wings as they climbed, and finally dared to open her eyes a crack.

She could only look down in awe as everything shrank as they climbed—the purple canyons, the emerald hills, and even the great redwood forest far off in the distance. Ara could see their shadow on the ground beneath them like that of a huge raptor, beating and gliding across the mottled green. Silwa was right; the air was cooler up here, and she was grateful for the blanket.

Ara held on, breathless, as her mind ceased thinking and worrying. A warmth spread from her heart down into her hands, and out into the liquid space around her. Wind streaming across her face, Ara flew with him, heart-first into the open. It felt effortless, limitless—like light soaking into her bones. Ara opened her mouth and a sound of joy escaped.

Ogran saw her and smiled before turning his attention back to the skies and their flying formation. The six took turns at riding in front and behind, Ara noted. She wanted to check on Petal and Lysander, but was afraid to open her bag, lest they got blown away. Instead, she focused on the steady warmth of the dragon beneath her hands, and the distant horizon, where a giant thunderhead stood outlined against the clear blue sky.

Nearly an hour later, they crossed over a series of craggy mountains and into a desert. The land beneath them now was red and dry, the vegetation sparse and unusually shaped, like sculpture. Somae signaled to a place below and the dragon began a slow and gradual descent, circling above a flat rock like a large red table thrusting a hundred feet or more from the Earth.

The dragon fanned his wings and dropped to the rock with a bounce, eliciting a little "oof" from Ara. She willed her chilled fingers to release their grip and looked around in wonder at the dramatic red-stone landscape.

The six kin landed in their diamond shape around the dragon, and Haru hurried over to check on him while Silwa addressed Ara.

"We'll stop here for a break and review our strategy. The tree is close," she said, before offering a hand.

Grateful, Ara took her warm hand and slid down the dragon's neck, letting herself drop the last step to the ground. Ara ran around to the dragon's face—she had to see his eyes and let him see her. "Thank you! That was incredible!" she gasped. The dragon snorted and blinked his acknowledgement.

She then remembered the insects were in her bag and opened it. Lysander streaked out, as if he'd been waiting for the first opportunity, while Petal paused at the opening to look around.

"*Good flying,*" she announced, after taking in the red stones and the sky.

"Where are we?" asked Ara, looking around at the odd rock formations and plants.

The air was quiet and still, and she could feel the heat flowing up from the ground. She scanned the horizon for clues of the whereabouts of the World Tree but only saw an uninterrupted expanse of red earth and deep blue sky. Larch was already inspecting a spiky plant and appeared to be gathering one of its flowers, while Sowelo had unwrapped the rest of their provisions and was spreading them on the ground.

"It's a desert—its name in our language means "sun-blasted," answered Silwa, regarding Ara thoughtfully.

Ara reached down to touch the dry, red earth, and then looked up at her. "It's beautiful! I've never seen land like this before. I know there's a part of Amethys like this, I've read about it, but I've spent my whole life in the forest, more or less," Ara replied.

Silwa simply nodded and strode off to join the others to talk strategy. Ara sat with them, eating from the leftovers and listening as they discussed what to do when they arrived at the tree. Petal and Lysander sat on the ground before Ara, listening.

"We need to see this army from the sky but remain unseen. We will then land at the roots, and gather our forces," Somae began.

"I will summon lightning, and torrential rains if needed," Sowelo said. The group nodded in agreement.

"And I will speak to the grasses—they will know the scope of the battlefield," said Larch.

Silwa raised her chin to her brother and Ogran. "We will be

ready to strike swiftly from the air. And with any luck, summon the Golden Walker, " she added.

Haru gave a long look to Eherion before turning back to the group. "And I will tend the dragon and ride him when he's ready to use fire."

Petal and Lysander floated to the middle of the circle so everyone could hear. "*And we will summon all of the small-winged creatures—the hornets, the wasps and all of the fearsome flyers!*" they declared.

Ara smiled as an image of the Citadel army overrun by hornets flashed through her mind.

The six looked at Ara. She wanted to contribute, but what powers did she have? Somae seemed to understand her worry.

"You are human, Ara, and know these people. You will be able to predict and sense what we cannot. Tell me—what weapons do they have?" he asked.

Ara swallowed. "They have velocraft—flying machines, and other rolling machines. And they have a giant drill that they'll try to use on the Tree. That's how they'll take its sap," she reported, feeling the heat rise in her face and seeing the looks of outrage on the faces of the kin.

"A drill?" exclaimed Haru, before she covered her own mouth.

Ara could only nod. They had no idea how powerful the Citadel was, nor how technologically advanced. Ara watched their faces harden, but a clear light shone through their eyes.

Silwa bowed her head and then looked up to address every-one. "Come, let us ride again. But this time, lower. Ogran, will you ride first?" she asked.

Ogran agreed, and as they assembled once more,

Ara offered the dragon some of her water. "*Are you thirsty? Or hungry?*" she asked, one hand upon his horn. It took Ara a little while to feel his answer.

"*No, I will not eat before battle. I don't know what will be asked of me,*" he replied.

"I think I understand. I don't want there to be a battle!" she sent.

"Nor do I. I don't want to hurt anyone. Humans are so soft and vulnerable," he answered back.

Ara realized that the six were all in position, waiting for her. She climbed on the dragon and called to Lysander and Petal, who nestled back into the bag.

As they took to the sky, Ara kept a hand on the dragon's horn. It was a bit of a reach, but she felt like she needed it to communicate with him.

After several minutes spent climbing with Ara clutching tightly with each downward beat of the dragon's wings, he caught an upward draft and spread them wide, coasting on a rapid current. Ara finally asked the question she'd had brewing in her mind since leaving the red rocks.

"That giant cloud—the thunderhead—is that the Tree?" she sent to the dragon as she studied the great green and blue thunderhead amassed on the horizon. It had to be tens of thousands of feet tall, its crown scraping the atmosphere. In one minute, it looked formless and soft like a cloud. But when a shaft of sunlight hit, it was solid, brown and green. A great wall of white cloaked part of the tree, and Ara could tell it was moving.

"Yes," came the dragon's reply, and Ara thought his voice sounded full of love.

Ara could almost feel his emotions as her own. It wasn't just a tree—it was a world.

With every beat of the dragon's wings, the Tree became larger, and more magnificent. Soon it had taken up her entire field of vision. Ara could see structures nestled into the Tree, and small lights traveling up and down along its bark.

Sowelo raised a hand from the front. The dragon beat his wings to slow their flight and Silwa yelled something to the other riders. Ara followed their gazes down to a long gray smudge on the ground. She squinted and could just make out little figures walking around in dark-green uniforms. Then she saw a long rectangle surrounded by a number of velocraft, some larger than she had ever seen before. It was the Citadel's army, just beyond the wall of mist. She shuddered and clutched the dragon tighter still.

Silwa let out a piercing whistle to the band, and the dragon beat his wings rapidly to slow their descent. The six landed one by one on a plain near the base of the great Tree. Ara and the dragon circled slowly before landing amidst them.

Gone was the view of the sky. Before them stood a wall of white mist, and behind them the massive wall of the Tree. Ara opened her bag to let Petal and Lysander fly free.

This time Ara went to look the dragon in the eyes first, before Haru. She wanted him to know her thanks. No matter what happened next, he had made her journey to the World Tree possible.

"Thank you," Ara said gently, as she patted his leathery face. The dragon let out a breath of warm air that reminded her of a horse's greeting. "And can I ask—what's your name?"

The dragon closed his eyes for several moments, and then blinked at her. Ara took that as her cue to listen through her hands and reached up to touch one of his horns.

"You have shown valor and your heart is pure. My name is Eherion. I am honored to have helped you, little one," he said.

"Thank you, Eherion!" Ara sent with a burst of her heartbeam.

Haru approached Eherion next and Ara stepped back to let her communicate with him. She could see Petal and Lysander, floating impatiently at her shoulder, ready to bring her to the Tree.

"Come!" sang Petal as she darted towards it. Ara glanced at Silwa, who placed a finger over her lips. Ara knew—the army was just across the plain, through the mist; any sounds they made would carry.

Slowly, silently, Ara walked to the World Tree. She lifted her hands to the bark and didn't need to summon the Greenspell. All of her thoughts went quiet as she bathed in its presence. Ara felt a tear of awe run down her cheek as her hands made contact.

The bark was warm, and Ara could have sworn it rippled beneath her hands. She absentmindedly wiped at the tear and touched the bark again.

"It's so...alive!" she whispered.

Petal and Lysander buzzed around her, and she knew they understood.

"*We must summon the winged ones now!*" Petal said, as she floated up the trunk of the tree with Lysander.

"*We'll be back!*" he called down to Ara, who waved at them from below.

"Ara!" whispered Silwa, calling her back to the group who were huddled over Larch; he had one hand on the ground.

As Ara drew closer, she could see that the grass beneath his hand had molded itself into shapes, and a detailed map of the Citadel army lay before them. Ara looked down in amazement—there were battalions and sections for machinery and ammunition. There were even tents! And there was a tally near the bottom, that read 20,000!

"It's best for us to summon our forces in the mist. Water and air are there, already together holding it in place. We need to enter," Silwa announced.

Larch had come to stand and Ogran was already peering at the wall of white before them. He adjusted his belt and Ara saw him touch the sword that hung there. Sowelo had a lethal look in her eyes as she rested both palms together at her forehead. Haru gazed at the mist head on, as if expecting something to come through it.

Instead of gazing at the mist, Ara closed her eyes and cast her mind as far as it would go. "They're moving," she said.

"What? You can feel them, Ara?" Silwa asked in alarm.

"Yes," Ara replied.

"Maybe I can help you find them," she added.

Silwa didn't question her further and simply nodded assent.

The group walked close together in near silence. Every step away from the Tree brought them closer to danger.

Ogran paused at the wall of mist, and then Ara watched him step within. Somae was just behind him, and Ara lost sight of him a moment later. She reached for Silwa's hand, close to hers, and breathed a sigh of relief when she grabbed hers back as they stepped through together. Larch, Haru and Sowelo followed.

Now they were all through, and Ara saw that Ogran and Somae, still in front, were looking around as if searching for something. He motioned for them to continue, and Ara squeezed Silwa's hand.

Ara walked hand in hand with Silwa in silence, deeper into the mist. With every step it felt like her ears were being filled with sheep's wool.

When they'd gone a bit further, Ara halted. She grabbed Silwa's elbow, and she stopped with her. She could just see the outline of her face and silver hair.

"Now I hear them," Ara whispered.

❧ 10 ☙

THE KEEPER HAD ARRIVED IN A VELOCRAFT TO THE SPRAWLING encampment that morning to see their progress for himself. He had dismounted from the craft, clutching the reports of the Tree's dimensions sent by his engineers in hand. When he'd seen the proposed radius, he balked. A new drill would need to be made, far bigger than had ever been created before. This would reach the core of the Tree and its precious sap. The Keeper only needed the smallest amount for himself, but no doubt it had many other uses.

He had found the army lively but bewildered. They couldn't understand why their instruments kept spinning, leaving them unable to locate the Tree with precision behind the mist. The Keeper had explained the situation as best as he could—that its size created a gravitational anomaly and that yes, it would be located, eventually—and let them grapple with the rest.

Even he had to admit that the mist was thick in this part of Onea. The small country had put up a fight several decades ago when Amethys had begun its expansion into empire, but no longer. None of his generals had mentioned anyone in the area save for a few farmers. And thanks to the Dark Spirit they had gotten as near as possible. Or as close as It could, the Keeper reminded himself. It had been one of the only times he had heard fear in Its voice as It had described that It would be annihilated if It touched the Tree; and so It had stayed away.

Looking into the miles-high wall of mist, the Keeper wondered if this might hold true for him as well. It was something he would explore in time, but certainly not today. For now, he stood back from the front line, which was suitable for a commander in battle. Hands clasped behind his back, he surveyed the groupings of soldiers. One group worked with heavy machines, another group flew small and large velocraft, while another had small platinum and copper arrows to be used if necessary.

"You there!" called the Keeper to a young soldier seated on a waiting velocraft.

The craft looked nimble; even if its instruments didn't work the fellow should be able to steer it correctly.

"Just fly straight through the mist and circle back once you've gotten close enough to see the Tree," he commanded.

The soldier gave a sharp nod but the Keeper noticed the look of disbelief in his eyes. Perhaps they had tried this approach before his arrival with an unmanned craft, but no one spoke.

The Keeper folded his arms as the velocraft lifted slowly from the ground. It shot forward with what should have been sufficient speed. The Keeper nearly groaned aloud with the men watching along beside him as the craft banked hard at a near ninety-degree angle and veered off to the left. The mist merely rippled after deflecting the craft. The Keeper turned away; they'd have to advance on the ground.

"Where?" Silwa asked, but Ara could only see her lips moving.

"Over there—" she pointed off to the right.

She heard the sounds of men muttering and squeaky wheels turning. A whole host of sounds filtered through to her.

Someone coughed and then someone far away laughed. Ara heard the sound of heavy boots on the ground. She strained to sense which direction they were coming from.

Silwa darted forward and brought back Somae and Ogran. They gestured to their ears and shook their heads. The entire group retreated to a safe distance and then Sowelo brought out her cauldron and placed it on the grass. Ara had the mad idea that she was about to make them tea when she reached up and grabbed a handful of air and placed it in the pot.

The other five lunged to the ground, one hand on the earth, one in the air and Ara felt the hair on the back of her neck rise. They began to whisper, one after another, with a sound like the pull of sand at the shore. The white wall of mist began to twist and coil around them. Thunder shook the ground beneath them and Ara watched as lightning crackled and branched through the mist.

Gasping, she crouched to the ground but the kin hadn't moved. Ara looked on in awe as a tall golden figure strode past them, tall as a house, lightning dripping from its hands. The Golden Walker...

The six jumped to their feet in joy, and Silwa strode to Ara, breathless. "This should slow their advance!" she said.

Ara felt a drop of rain on her shoulder. And then another.

"Quick—let's take to the air before the deluge," cried Somae.

"Ara—hurry to the Tree. It won't be raining there," Silwa said.

Silwa had a short discussion with Haru before turning back to the mist. Ara held out a hand, unsure if she were saying good-bye. What if they were injured in battle? And how would she know?

"We'll hold them at bay," Silwa began, already reading her thoughts. "We aim for the machines, not the men. We will move quickly and disable them—and may you find the Seed!" she whispered fiercely, before flying off with the other four kin.

Ara watched them disappear into the mist, and her ears picked up a new sound above the booming thunder—the faraway drone of millions of insects approaching the battlefield. Ara smiled to herself; the small-winged ones had heeded the call. It was time for her to find the Seed. With the battle underway, this might be the only chance she would get. Did the World Tree drop its seeds on the ground? Or were they high above in the branches?

Ara and Haru began to walk back to Eherion and the Tree. Ara took a step on the grass, eyes forward, and felt something shift around them. The back of her neck began to tingle and she had the sense that someone—or something— was watching. Ara turned to Haru, mouth open to speak.

"Sir, the mist is changing!" called a young soldier from farther down the line.

The Keeper whipped his head around to locate the shift. At first, he saw nothing. And then the wall of white deepened in color. The front line recoiled slightly at the change, and he took a step forward. What was it that he felt?

Like a sudden avalanche, a wall of thunder roared towards them and lightning shot from the mist.

The Keeper held up a hand. "Hold your fire!" he called along the line.

There was a sharp intake of breath behind him as the archers shuddered to obey his command. This level of magic was not human.

He walked forward across the field to the very edge of the mist, his hand still raised to halt all weapons. There was something before him. Was it the one who had summoned this illusion? Or was it someone else...?

The Keeper continued his slow walk until the sounds of the army behind him had faded. He sent his mind beyond the mist, probing, searching as the lightning buzzed and cracked in the air all around.

The Keeper watched in awe as a great golden being strode forward. He felt the blood drain from his face as he realized that it was immortal. It looked across the field to a distant location, seemingly unconcerned with the thousands of men at its feet. It began to walk with purpose, and the Keeper relaxed a fraction. It seemed to have its own plans.

Then the rain began. At first, it was just a spatter. But then great sheets of water lashed the air. The Keeper was drenched, and still he couldn't tear his eyes from something within the mist...

There. She was right over there—his beacon beyond the wall.

He turned on his heel and retreated back to his front line. The Keeper barely saw the looks of awe on the faces of the soldiers he passed, as they'd seen him walk through a thunderstorm in full gale.

He found the nearest archer. "Aim. Right. There." The Keeper pointed to where she was.

The archer took a few moments to get his aim correct and let fly.

The Keeper heard a hiss of pain and then a thwack as the arrow hit home. He rested a hand on the young archer's shoulder. "Well done—now we have our mark," he said.

As he stood, he considered finding the girl himself and thought better of it. He didn't want to get too close to the Tree.

"You two," he said, pointing to two hardened soldiers nearby. "There's a girl through the mist, at the Tree. Go find her and bring her to me!"

Ara heard the platinum arrow whizz past. Haru gasped beside her, as it pierced her outstretched wing and sank deep into the Tree with a thud. All of the blood drained from Ara's face as Haru stumbled to one knee, wincing.

"Haru! Haru! Are you ok?" she cried, as she tried to pull her up from the ground. Her right wing hung limply and Ara could see a small piece of it was missing. Haru's face was a mask of pain, but her voice was calm.

"Ara—bring me to Eherion," she said.

Ara lifted Haru as gently as she could and helped her walk to the dragon. The mist seemed to be getting thicker as the rain fell steadily around them, but Ara could still make out his large purple form. She could also hear the sounds of men's voices through the mist, and they were getting closer.

"Thank you. I'll be alright, little sister," Haru said, taking a few steps on her own.

Happy to see her stride forward, Ara hung back, ready to grab her elbow or hand if she needed.

Eherion lifted his head and Ara watched him smell the air. The mist was definitely moving closer, but what did that mean?

Ara was mid-step when she felt the air tighten and constrict around her. She landed on the ground with a thud and felt herself being pulled backwards. "Haru?! Eherion!" she called.

The grass scratched against her face as she cried out for help and thrashed within the net as it pulled taut. Four hands lifted her up from behind, and she saw the face of one of the Citadel soldiers. Eyes cold, he muttered, "A wily one, aren't you?" before the four hands lifted her and placed her on something flat.

Ara looked on in horror as the Keeper eyed her calmly from his pilot's chair. She was next to him, in a velocraft. Through the black net she could see that it was small with low walls. Gone were the Keeper's flowing robes, replaced by a snug suit of black and green. He touched some instruments and Ara felt the velocraft lift.

"You can't take me back to the Citadel!" she cried at him.

Ara felt the craft waver in the air a moment and then lurch forward. The Keeper turned to look at her, and his gaze told her he saw a miserable clump of girl in a net. He turned away but Ara kept railing.

"I know what you're doing! I know about the drill! Well, it

won't work. The Tree has protection!" she cried, as she desperately tried to free her hands and the heavy black webbing that obscured her vision.

She felt the velocraft shift again beneath them. Were they climbing?

Ara changed position in the net and started to work on the knots at her feet. She had gotten one undone when the velocraft veered suddenly and she was given a view of the ground. Whisps of mist floated in the air, but she could see that the Citadel army was moving backwards, away from the Tree. Something in the distance was on fire. Ara could only pray it was the drill. A large purple dragon circled above the land, searching. "Eherion!" she cried.

Ara might as well have been invisible for all the attention the Keeper paid her. He stayed silent for several moments more and Ara had to wonder where they were headed. If he were taking her back to the Citadel to be reprimanded, shouldn't they have left the battlefield? Instead they kept climbing.

Now she felt the wind blowing around her as she had on Eherion, and her heart began to ache. Would Haru be alright? Were Silwa and the band really winning? *"Please, please don't let them hurt Eherion!"* she prayed.

Bright green leaves passed by at eye level from where she lay on the floor of the velocraft. They had only to climb a few more feet before she understood his plan.

The Keeper turned to her. "I'm afraid you've seen too much," he announced, as he leaned over her and braced his feet against the floor of the velocraft.

She'd just finished the last knot in the net, and yanked it over her head. Ara tried to grab anything at hand—anything at all— but her hands met with only the smooth metal floor.

"Goodbye," the Keeper said softly, giving her a powerful shove out of the velocraft.

% II %

ARA SHRIEKED BUT FELT THE AIR IN HER LUNGS FREEZE SOLID as she plummeted. She had her hands splayed out, searching for something to grab. Time slowed but she fell faster, looking at the darkening blue sky above. The first stars were just starting to come out, and their light seemed to follow her descent.

Suddenly, Ara felt something firm cradle her from below. It was strong but flexible, and it didn't so much stop her as slow her gradually.

"I've got you," spoke a deep voice in her mind.

Ara wiped away the tears that had been streaming down her face, unnoticed. She'd floated to a stop amidst many branches and leaves. She touched the branch closest to her and sent a pulse from her heartbeam.

"Thank you! Is it really you? Are you the World Tree?!" she sent through her hand.

"It is and I am. I would never let one such as you fall. You shed a tear of gratitude for me. And no tears of yours shall be wasted," replied the Tree.

Ara sat up, dumbstruck in the nest the Tree had created just for her, formed from its powerful branches that now appeared as gnarled wooden hands.

"Do you know what's happening down there? Are the Elementals winning?" Ara asked. There was a long pause, as if the Tree were watching the ground.

"There is much chaos, but yes...they are winning. For now," said the Tree.

Ara let out the breath she'd been holding. The stars seemed brighter now and Ara noticed faint lines of light flowing out from the top of the tree. They were slender, gleaming threads in gold, green, blue, and lavender. Each one connected to a distant point of light, far above in the night sky. There were threads that connected to each of the constellations she recognized—the Bear, the Seven Sisters, the Hunter. There was a surge of blue from one very bright star and Ara watched in awe as its light pulsed and shimmered down to the tree and its waiting branches below.

"Are you talking to the stars?!" she asked.

"All the time. We are in constant communication," came the reply.

Ara sat back in her perch and marveled at the view, as the Tree sent and received little pulses of light through its branches to the stars and back again. No wonder the Tree was so powerful, so revered. It was like a cosmic lighthouse.

"Indeed. I am connected to all that is," it answered in the silence.

"Can you help me? Can I have the Flaming Seed, to take back with me to the Citadel?" she asked.

Ara tried to explain the larger story of why she was there. The Tree listened and then spoke again in its deep bass voice:

"I have waited for a human as brave and alive as you are, Ara. My seeds are within. They were scattered to many corners of the Earth, long ago. They are rare, but I give them freely..." said the Tree.

"Oh, thank you! Thank you!" Ara sent and realized that the Tree already knew her name.

"Let me show you more about the Flame—what it really is," the Tree said.

Ara wasn't sure how it would do that, but soon a very clear

image popped into her mind. It felt like the Tree, so she didn't move her hand.

Ara saw the original Flame at the Citadel, burning brightly. There were many people standing around it, with smiles on their faces. And then she was looking at the same scene, but from above, outside the Citadel. Then she was pulled higher and higher into the sky.

Now she could see thousands of small lights glowing all over the world, each one connected to the Tree like a candle placed on its branches. And Ara saw that they were all connected to each other. Each one was like a window into all the others. And through each one the Tree could see everyone as well. Every face that gazed into a flame was known.

The Tree pulled her higher still until she could see its full size, stretching up to the stars and planets, and all of the tiny balls of light on the ground below.

"Do you see now? This is why, at the Citadel, it is said to be a flame of knowledge. For if you use the Flame as it is meant to be—like a window, or portal to the universe—much wisdom and knowledge may find you," spoke the Tree.

"Oh..." was all Ara could muster.

The scale of the interconnection of lights and knowing was nearly unfathomable.

"And it is for everyone; not just the Order," added the Tree.

"Okay..." Ara replied. "I think I understand better now."

If everyone had this knowledge, they wouldn't need the Order, Ara thought.

She felt the hands begin to move her very slowly through the air, until she was right against the bark. A doorway appeared, and Ara's face was washed in bright golden light.

"There is one who lives here and tends my roots. She has been waiting for you as well," said the Tree.

From the doorway floated a golden orb. Ara recognized it immediately as the golden orb she'd seen in the forest at the

Citadel; the one that had given her the Greenspell. It shimmered and Ara felt a bubble of laughter rise from her belly.

The golden orb retreated to the doorway and Ara understood that she was to follow.

"It's alright, you won't fall within. You'll float," the Tree said.

Ara gave the hands that had caught her a grateful pat before stepping through the doorway after the golden orb, which now floated above a disc within the tree. Ara gazed around at the bright light that shone from the walls, which were a beautiful golden honeycomb.

Together, they drifted down slowly, gently the full length of the Tree. Ara had no sense of time passing, but when they finally reached the bottom, she could only see the golden shaft of light that seemed to reach far, far above.

The orb traveled down a winding corridor that Ara took to be a root and led her into a chamber. Ara looked around in wonder.

She now stood in a large round room made of wood, with many glowing lamps of different colors. The golden orb had floated to the center, where it lengthened into a radiant egg.

The light gradually faded, and a small person stood before her in its place, glowing with a soft blue light. The person had a very old face, and slightly pointy ears. They held up a hand in greeting and smiled gently. Ara looked into the deep black eyes, and the face that reminded her of a wizened apple.

"Great, great, great many times grandmother," said the figure in a magical, bird-like voice, touching her heart.

Ara's mind nearly stopped altogether. "You're—you're my grandmother?" she asked in a whisper. The figure nodded.

"I have seen many children, as I watch from here, in the Tree," she said in explanation.

Ara could feel that her shock had softened, but not by much. "And you're human?" she asked, as she saw her delicate wings of orange.

The black eyes crinkled. "Yes, yes...that I am," she replied. "I've waited long for you," she said, and gave Ara a radiant smile that reached every wrinkle of her face.

Ara looked at her bashfully.

"I am Naia. I watch since you were a baby, and I see your progress," she said, eyes twinkling.

Ara's heart swelled at the idea of her watching from afar.

"I sent the insects to find you, wake you up," she said, and then giggled to herself. "And I made sure you had this," she said, gesturing to the vines at Ara's wrists.

"Now you're here, I will show you what you need to know," she said, pulling Ara by the hand to another part of the room. Her grasp was warm and strong, and Ara could feel how long her fingers were.

Ara's tiny grandmother stopped before a large oval mirror covered in a golden cloth. Ara hadn't noticed it before, nor had she seen the plentiful tray of food that had materialized on the table nearby.

"Look!" said her grandmother, gesturing to the mirror.

Ara stood blinking into the looking glass. Unlike a normal mirror, its surface swirled like molten silver. It slowly crystallized and she could see the room, and her small face, crowned with a cloud of hair. A pair of turquoise wings, edged with green and gold grew from her back. They came to two rounded points about a foot above her shoulders and the same distance below her hips, like a butterfly.

"I... I have wings too?" she asked in awe.

Ara cast her eyes to her shoulders and saw nothing. Ever so carefully she reached out to touch them, following their outline in the mirror; she could almost convince herself that she felt them, like a soft buzz in the air beneath her fingertips.

"Yes, yes...not visible but there all the same," Naia said, nodding.

Ara's face broke into a smile of wonder. She had wings! She

let her eyes take in every detail. "Does this mean I can fly?" she asked.

Naia laughed. "No, no," she replied.

Ara's face fell and Naia pulled on her hand again. "No matter, no matter. All humans have wings, visible or invisible; I'm just showing yours to you now," she said and drew Ara to the tray of food and nearby stools.

She gestured for Ara to sit and she sat opposite. "You have my necklace, then?" she asked, pointing towards Ara's chest.

Ara frowned and touched the cord at her neck. "You mean— this necklace?!"

She pulled the talisman over her head and held it out for her tiny grandmother to see. It hung between them in the air, smooth and brown.

"Yes!" Naia said, beaming. "I knew you'd have it!" she exclaimed.

Ara watched in surprise as Naia kissed the etching of the tree in the stone. "You survived," she whispered to the stone in her palm. "It is mine, passed down in our family for many genera-tions!" Naia added with a quick look at Ara.

"Grandma gave it to me when I turned twelve! She said it was special, but..." Ara trailed off. Something about the way Naia held it told Ara there was more to learn. "What kind of stone is it, anyway?" she asked.

Naia cackled softly. "Stone? This is no stone! It's a seed from the Tree." Her dark eyes danced with light as she stroked the talisman. "It just needs awakening," she whispered.

Ara felt a shiver of recognition at her words. "It's a *seed?* I've had a seed from the World Tree this whole time?!" she exclaimed. But Naia was no longer listening.

Naia held the talisman in a cupped hand beneath her mouth. She closed her eyes and as the first notes fell from her lips, Ara felt all of the hairs on her body stand on end. Images blossomed in her mind. She saw stars and faces and a small green tree bursting from the land. It grew larger and stronger with every new strand that was added to the musical braid. All of a sudden, the talisman seemed to catch fire beneath the song, and Ara gasped as a faint light rippled over its surface in a rainbow of colors.

Naia finally opened her eyes, still holding the last note of the song. Looking pleased, she nodded imperceptibly at the seed glowing in her hand and held it out to Ara. "You see—the Flaming Seed! Carry it close as you did before," she instructed.

Grasping it gently, Ara closed her hands together and brought an eye close to peer within the darkness she'd created. The Seed still glowed, casting lights within the space of her hands. "The Flaming Seed!" she echoed in wonder. "And what did you sing to it?" she asked.

"That's the Tree's original song, from when it first came upon the Earth. I sing that song to it now as I tend the roots, to keep it healthy," Naia explained.

"I saw those images in my mind, from when the tree was younger!" Ara said.

Naia simply nodded and gestured for her to put it on.

Ara bowed her head as she settled it over her shoulders. She placed a hand on its familiar contour beneath her sweater, feeling its warmth and imagining the light it cast on her chest. It felt right there; it had been with her all along but now it was alive.

"Hmm, yes. Bring back with you. And now for your teacher," Naia declared, getting up from her seat.

Ara had to hurry to follow Naia as she led Ara deeper into the root tunnels, patting the sides of the walls and singing a little song as she walked. Ara thought her motions were very fast for someone so ancient.

At last, she led her to a still pool of water, its surface black.

"How do you know about Tobias?" Ara asked her.

"I healed him once and have been watching him ever since. A good boy. And a steward of the forest," she replied.

"Wow..." muttered Ara, as she took in this new connection.

Naia gestured for Ara to come closer and grabbed a large horn that sat on a ledge beside the pool. She dipped the horn into the water and Ara saw thousands of stars come to life in the darkness.

"Sacred well, to feed the roots. These waters will heal Tobias, but he can no longer be a bird, only a man," Nana said, holding out a horn filled to the brim with shimmering clear water.

Ara hurriedly drew her waterskin from her pack, drained it and refilled it with the sacred waters.

Naia hummed her approval as she resealed it and placed it safely away. "Only for him—no one else," she said. Ara heard the strength in her voice and nodded.

"Lastly—you must free she that sleeps beneath. A venerable water dragon below the Citadel, soon to be waking. Go there first and use the Greenspell to free her." Naia's black eyes bore into Ara's as if she were giving her additional silent instructions.

"A dragon lies beneath the Citadel?" she questioned.

"Yes, of course. It is an ancient seat of power on Earth; that is where they dwell—the dragons... The Citadel once held many things in balance, in connection," she said, wistful.

Ara didn't know what she had done to deserve these gifts, and these teachings. She wanted to ask but didn't know how. Naia seemed to read this in her eyes.

"Your heart is strong. And you understand togetherness. All things are interconnected," she said clearly. Ara heard her words —felt them, even—with every cell of her body.

"When you return, tell your family about me. About us," she said and gestured to the roots of the Tree all around them.

Ara closed her eyes, and tried to envision telling her parents and her grandmother about the wonders she'd seen, and Naia. Would they understand?

"Okay, I'll do my best. At least Grandma will believe me," she replied.

Naia looked to the ceiling and laughed. Ara wasn't sure what was so funny about trying to explain all of this to them, but she laughed along with her.

Naia wiped her eyes and gave her a warm but serious look. "It's time. The roots of this Tree travel far. I will bring you back," she said finally.

"But—will I see you again? And what about Silwa and everyone else?" Ara asked. Her mind flitted to Eherion, and Petal and Lysander.

Naia smiled as if seeing her thoughts. "If you wish it, you will," she said warmly, looking at her with what she recognized to be love. Ara knew this to be true, but she didn't know how it would come to pass.

Naia took her hands again and Ara felt the Greenspell come to life. She led her down one of the root tunnels, past the sacred well. Her many-times great-grandmother gave her a wink and pulled Ara forward with an otherworldly power.

They flew hand in hand with great speed through the roots like a drop of water, and Ara felt her ears pop as the root tunnel narrowed around them. She saw tiny pinpricks of gold and lavender in the walls and knew it was the same web of life, the mycelium, she'd seen before.

They might have traveled for minutes, or hours, Ara couldn't tell for sure. But at last, the rushing in her ears ceased and they floated to a stop. Her tiny grandmother pointed to a stone door before them. Upon it was a symbol Ara recognized.

"We're at the Citadel?!" she asked, incredulous.

Naia nodded without taking her gaze from the spiral carved into the door. "Yes—deep underground, where the magic still lives. Past this door is an old hall, and there you will find the dragon," she said.

Naia let go of Ara's hands and then made her check that she had the Seed and the sacred water for Tobias. And then she took a step backwards. "This is as far as I can go; I must stay within the Tree," she announced.

"Okay," answered Ara back, breathless.

Naia gave a little wave and Ara watched her form return to that of the golden orb. Wiping a tear from her cheek, she turned from her tiny grandmother, who had just begun to float backwards, to the door just beyond the root. Naia's light still lit the way, and with one last look at the orb, she pushed the door open with all her might.

Ara walked through the door and stepped between two pillars. Before her stretched a vast space. Giant columns of quartz soared overhead and burst into glittering fragments at the ceiling, casting a pale, milky light on the chamber below. The air was cool and thick and left a tangy taste in Ara's mouth.

She stood in awe, one hand still on the column beside her. It looked like a twin to the Great Hall above, frozen in the distant past. *How could this have been kept secret?* she wondered, as she ventured closer to the nearest wall. The part near the floor was covered in colorful paintings.

Peering closer, Ara could see groups of people and animals surrounded by flowers and vines. There were cat people, and tall blue birds; regular looking people and even, Ara noted with a faint smile, the human Elementals with wings. And there were dragons in the air above them, circling.

Now to find and free the water dragon, Ara thought.

Feeling like an ant amidst a hall made for giants, she sped across the stone floor, her feet just visible in the light. Ara crossed through the center and felt her feet brush against something smooth. She knelt down and grazed the ground with her fingertips. She could just make out an intricate pattern inlaid in the floor in metal, or was it glass? She had a strange feeling that she was now standing directly below the Flame.

Ara's head whipped around as she saw the larger pattern of the black, glossy substance. It was in the shape of the Flame, reminding her of the talisman the Keeper had given to Geera. And she now recognized it as a seal of dark magic, similar to the seal that had been placed on Silwa and the band in the Treeways.

"BOOM!"

A sound like thunder shook the floor of the hall and Ara was thrown backwards. She who slept beneath.

"*BOOM!*"

The second jolt of the hall knocked Ara to the ground where she rolled several feet away as the floor tilted beneath her.

Ara got to her feet and ran to the very center of the seal. Steadying herself, she willed the Greenspell to life. A golden light surged beneath her hands, followed by a fizzing sound as the dark seal began to melt away.

"*Stand back!*" came a clear, authoritative voice into Ara's mind.

Spotting a set of crystal thrones at the base of a column she quickly ran to them. After a spilt second of hesitation, she clambered behind one of them, and peered around its back.

Bright blue light began to radiate from the ground. It widened, and widened and Ara felt the light on her face. She was just about to scurry back further when a great surge of water erupted from the floor, soaring high into the air, nearly grazing the ceiling.

From within the light, a form began to materialize, turning, twisting, until the full body of the water dragon was complete and free. It flew in loops around the hall, mouth opening and closing as if drinking in the air. Ara clutched the throne tightly, her jaw open in wonder as she watched the water dragon flip and spin.

Eventually the dragon came to a soft landing above the center of the hall and pawed at the broken seal. It tilted its head to the sky and then rained down a torrent of blue flame while Ara cowered behind the tall back of the throne. The light made her think of the light of the original Flame, which had been a glorious blue. The dragon sat on its hind legs, its long neck now in a relaxed curve, its eyes calm and blinking as it looked about the chamber, then down at the thrones.

"*It is safe now—are you going to come out?*" said the dragon in her mind.

Slowly prising her hands from the chair, Ara climbed down

and stood beside it. She looked up at the face of the water dragon whose large blue eyes looked down at her with equal amounts of warmth and ferocity. Ara wondered how she could hear her so clearly, without having to touch her. Maybe she was getting stronger.

"Thank you for releasing me! I have slept long in my home in the mountain beneath this hall and awoke to find myself imprisoned... A most unpleasant experience. Even if I could travel in other ways, my physical essence was bound," she said, sighing deeply.

The dragon lowered her head to address Ara. *"In honor of your service, I will give you my name. I am Ixytria. And you are...?"*

Ara swallowed and took a step forward. "I am Ara. My ancestor Naia told me you were here. I'm so glad I could help!" she said aloud. Ara drew closer to her giant blue paws. It looked like water was running down her forelegs but the stone floor remained dry. Ixytria peered around her at the walls, and the ceiling.

"Where is the sun? I don't remember darkness such as this," Ixytria said in a whisper.

"It's still here—but far, far above. There's another hall on top of this one. In fact, there's a whole massive building on top of it!" Ara exclaimed.

How long had she been sleeping, Ara wondered, to have missed the building of the Citadel?

"Ahh..." said the water dragon, closing her eyes. *"I see. It has been an age. My sleep cycle lasts close to twelve thousand years. The others must be awakening too—though I hope to far better circum-stances,"* she added calmly as if twelve thousand years were simply a matter of months.

She sat very still for a few minutes, and Ara watched her chest move up and down, and her great blue wings lift and fall. She didn't want to interrupt her, but she didn't know how much time she'd have. Had the Keeper returned from the World Tree yet?

"Ixytria?" Ara whispered.

The blue dragon fluttered her eyes open. *"I was just listening, to see if any other dragons are awake, and nearby,"* she answered.

Ara stepped closer. "There is one! A fire dragon named Eherion. He let me ride him to the World Tree!" she exclaimed. Ixytria looked down at her intently.

"Where is he? And how did it come to pass?" she asked.

Ara told her the entire story, beginning with her suspicions that something was wrong with the Flame. She ended by patting the necklace at her chest. "And I have it now—the Flaming Seed. I just need to find my teacher, Tobias, then figure out how to get into the Great Hall to relight it!"

Ixytria had come to her full height while listening to Ara's tale. And now she extended her wings all the way, and Ara saw her eyes smolder.

"Then I will join the others at the World Tree now and protect it. But before I go, I will lay the path forward for you, Ara. I will extinguish the false flame and create a portal to a place of great light. You must get this Keeper to stand within it—and whatever darkness resides in him shall flow out and up through the portal to be transmuted back to light. This will vanquish it once and for all—it will not escape. That will be my justice," she said.

Ara bowed her head deeply in thanks. *If only it could be that simple,* she thought. Maybe, if she could find Tobias fast enough, and gather a team together. She would need to be in the Great Hall without the Keeper and professors around.

"I will help you find your teacher, not far from here," she said, sniffing the air, and looking up at the ceiling high above. Ara waited as she scanned the area, searching and feeling with her dragon senses. She grunted and blew out through her nostrils.

"He's in a small cell, a few levels above this one. There are two, right next to each other," she said, closing her eyes. *"But one is a trap. You will know the correct one by its silence."*

Ixytria lengthened her neck and then curled it close to where Ara stood, so her head was almost level with her own. *"Here,"* she said, and nipped lightly at her broad chest. She drew something angular away and placed it on the ground before Ara. Her skin rippled for a moment and she shook herself like a dog.

Ara approached the scale carefully. It was an iridescent blue, in the same pattern of a snakeskin. Grasping it gently with her fingertips, Ara felt how cool and heavy it was, and solid like a crystal. It felt like nothing she had ever touched in her life.

"*This will turn metal to water—you may use it to melt the lock,*" Ixytria instructed.

"Thank you!" Ara replied, placing it in one of her pockets for safe-keeping.

Ara blanched at the thought of a trap being laid for her, or anyone who went to find him. But given everything she knew now, it made sense. Then she thought of everyone above—Nat, Ember, Geera—and had a question.

"Ixytria—before you leave—can you show yourself to the people in the Citadel?" Ara asked. They had to know she was real, that dragons were real.

"*Don't worry, dear. When I have finished in the Great Hall, all will know of my presence,*" she said, satisfaction in her voice.

Ixytria shifted her legs and stretched her massive blue wings. Ara felt her energies expand and took an instinctive step backwards as the light around her began to swirl and then meld into a powerful beam.

"*Let us leave this hall,*" Ixytria said, as her taloned feet left the floor. "*And free the waters once more.*"

Ara wanted to run towards her, but only managed to raise a hand.

Ixytria floated above in her full magnificence, rising slowly along the column of light, the tips of her wings brushing the ceiling above.

"*Farewell, Ara! And fear nothing. You have everything you need!*" she said, before disappearing into the column in a flash of blue brilliance.

Ara shielded her eyes as a gale-force wind pushed her backwards. She could have sworn she heard her whisper something in her mind as she left, long soft syllables like a blessing in an ancient language.

Ara stood for a few moments in the abandoned hall, feeling the hush left in Ixytria's absence before sprinting for the stairs at the far wall. With her feet on the final step, and the lowest level of the Citadel now spread before her, she looked back one last time to the abandoned hall. It had revealed more than she could have imagined. Ara prayed that Ixytria would do all she said, and join Eherion.

Now to find Tobias.

The Keeper settled himself in his favorite chair, exhausted and happy to be alone once more in his chambers. He'd returned from his short-lived flight with the girl to a scene of chaos on the battlefield below. He'd circled once before landing to get a clearer picture for himself, before receiving a briefing from one of his captains on the ground.

The drill had been partially melted, and the machines used to transport it destroyed. The captain had insisted that a tall golden being had strode from the mist and then continued past the army before circling back several minutes later.

The Keeper had frowned at the man to continue his tale, but knew he spoke the truth.

Then, apparently, a group of flying people had harried the archers and made off with some provisions only to have a wall of hornets and wasps force most of the army under the cover of the largest velocraft.

This ridiculous account made the Keeper turn on his heel —but only after he assured the captain that he would return with any necessary reinforcements and a much, much larger drill.

A pad of paper before him on his desk, he began to calculate what was needed to finish the job. He planned to meet with both the Inner and the Outer Councils that very evening, and he wanted to be ready.

A quiet knock sounded at the door. He wasn't expecting anyone, but perhaps a servant was bringing tea. He ignored the knock until he heard a muffled, "Sir?" from behind the door.

"What is it?" he hissed, recognizing the worried tone in Professor Nirla's voice.

"In the Great Hall, Sir. I think you'd better come look. There's...a disturbance of sorts. Well—it's raining!" reported Nirla through the door.

The Keeper put down his pencil. He crossed the room and joined Nirla in the hallway. Together, they walked in silence for several moments.

"Did you bar the doors?" he asked Nirla as they turned down the last corridor.

"Yes—all but one. But I think some of the students got quite an eyeful anyway," he muttered darkly.

As they drew closer, Nirla motioned to one of the guards stationed at a closed door to open it and step aside. The Keeper quickly read the look of fear on the man's face and gave him a withering stare.

As the guard fumbled with the door mechanisms, the Keeper scanned the hallway for passersby. There were a few clumps of students stationed at different points along the corridor. With his preternatural senses he could hear them whispering excitedly amongst themselves.

The Keeper recognized the face and voice of the persistent boy who'd kept after him about dragons. His eyes were wide and he gestured vehemently to a girl standing nearby. The sweating guard opened the door, and he swept in with Nirla in his wake.

The Keeper advanced to the center of the room, ignoring the lashings of rain that fell from a miniature storm cloud high above, just below the ceiling. He took in the bare podium where the Flame had once stood, where now just a blue cup sat on the floor. Circling around the room like a blazing comet was a dragon. Glorious and blue, her sheer size and power left him breathless for a moment. Nirla stood next to him, quaking and sodden. The Keeper noticed a golden light in the far end of the hall, streaming down as if from a mysterious sun.

"Sir—is that a dragon?!" Nirla whispered.

The Keeper ignored him and called upon the Dark Spirit. It was supposed to have sealed her away for good.

His call was answered, and in spite of Its protestations that It had done what he asked, It really had, the Dark Spirit made good on Its promise to expel her.

The Keeper let his power build and build as the rain continued to fall down around them. And then he struck her with his mind, like a metal hammer. The dragon recoiled backwards and then flew up and out of the Hall through the ceiling in a jet of blue mist.

"A demon, not a dragon," he whispered back to Nirla. "But it's been defeated now, not to worry. See that this Hall remains closed and guarded for the time being, at the very least until our meeting tonight. And stifle any talk of dragons that arises..." he added, before turning to leave.

"But, sir! What about the Flame? How can it be relit?" questioned Nirla with worried eyes.

He was a good deputy, and knew the larger plan, but the Keeper had forgotten that he knew nothing of the Flame's falseness. He paused to consider.

The Dark Spirit, which had been rather remote since his visit to the World Tree, provided him with the perfect answer. He marveled that he hadn't thought of it before.

"The Flame is easy to relight. This is sacred knowledge, passed down from one Keeper to the next. I was told that one simply needs to retrieve a seed from the World Tree to light it once more..." he trailed off.

The Keeper saw a flash of recognition pass through Nirla. "We can tell the Councils—all the more reason why we must access the Tree immediately!" he hissed.

"Precisely," replied the Keeper. He motioned with his head for them to move away. The rain had stopped with the dragon's departure; an eerie calm filled the Hall and their footsteps seemed to echo more loudly than before.

The Dark Spirit was now yelling in his ear as they walked. Under no circumstances could he approach the golden light, still shining down in one corner of the Hall—and so he gave it a wide berth before striding out, still wet.

ARA STEPPED INTO THE COOL, MOIST AIR OF THE TUNNEL, which led to a warren of doors within the curved stone walls. She hadn't thought the Citadel had dungeons but clearly, she'd been wrong.

A torch glowed like a beacon, far in the distance. Ara sped towards it through the darkness, her eyes adjusting quickly to the change. She willed the Greenspell alive and touched the smooth walls at intervals, letting her hands sense what they could as she cast her mind forward in space, looking for Tobias.

As Ara neared the dancing flame, she collected whisps of information from the stones. These chambers had once been used for healing, like hermits' caves. She sensed a deep peace at odds with their current use. Ara shivered and drew her hands away from one spot on the wall that spoke to that reality.

She paused when she reached the torch marking an intersection of tunnels up ahead. Would Tobias be guarded? Ara closed her eyes again to concentrate. *"Tobias?!"* she called from her heart. *"Where are you?"*

No response came.

Ara couldn't feel anyone behind her and guessed that all human activity was now before her. Taking a chance, Ara popped her head around the corner beneath the torch. A long, curved hallway with several stout doors spread in two directions before branching into darkness once again. He was here. One door called to her, just out of reach of the light.

Ara stood like a wild animal, sensing and feeling, eyes open and then closed, while a bead of sweat rolled down her back from between her shoulder blades. A muffled cough issued from the door to the right, followed by a heart-wrenching sigh.

Thank you, Ixytria, thought Ara, as she turned away and walked to the last door. She placed her ear against it but could hear nothing from the chamber within.

She eyed the crude metal lock interlaced through the stone door. She took the scale from her pocket and pressed it over the lock, hoping this was what Ixytira had meant her to do. There was a hissing as the cold metal began to bubble and drip on the floor. Ara nearly dropped the scale before she realized that the metal was indeed like water, and cool to the touch.

She grasped the lock and with another satisfying twist felt it yield completely. She quickly pocketed the scale, which seemed to still be intact, and placed the mangled lock on the floor.

A small, jagged window now opened into the cell beyond. It lay in near total darkness, save for a solitary candle, whose light just grazed the outline of a figure on the ground.

Ara pushed the door open and two golden hawk eyes snapped open from within the darkness at the sound. "Tobias? It's me, it's Ara!" she whispered as she took a step inside.

"Ara! How? Is that really you?" came the familiar voice.

"Yes, Tobias, it's me! I'm here to free you!" she said softly, taking a few more steps towards the giant bird.

Tobias flapped his wings and walked towards her. His head turned from the door and back to her in a bird-like fashion, his singular eyes the only indicator that he was more than a hawk.

"I have so many questions, Ara, starting with how you opened the lock. But they'll have to wait. The Keeper might return to check on me at

any time. And I don't want him to find you. What is your plan?" he asked.

Ara was moved by his immediate concern for her well-being. He was the one who had been trapped there, and no doubt wanted nothing more than to return to his home in the forest.

"I must go to the Great Hall and relight the Flame—and tell everyone who the Keeper really is and what he's done," Ara replied.

Tobias blinked his golden eyes once and Ara could feel his unspoken thoughts.

She patted her necklace. "I have the Flaming Seed here, and a gift for you from my ancestor at the World Tree," she whispered in response.

Tobias closed his eyes. *"You did it, Ara!"*

Ara held out her waterskin. For a second, she could have sworn she felt the presence of her tiny great grandmother, standing behind her.

"This water is from a sacred well at the World Tree. My ancestor Naia tends the roots there, and she cared for you long ago after your battle with the Keeper. She said these waters will heal you completely. But that you will no longer be able to turn into a bird and stay only a man."

Ara felt the words flow from her mouth like an oracle and saw a quickening in Tobias's golden eyes. She knew she had hit a nerve with the mention of the one who had tended him long ago.

"The one who healed me?!" was all he could say.

She pushed the waterskin an inch closer and held it level with his beak. "And she told me how she has watched you, ever since," she added.

Ara almost repeated what Naia had said about him being a good boy.

"Thank you," he whispered. *"This is a gift...beyond my wildest imaginings,"* he said. *"But I will not change form yet. Something tells me*

I can be more useful like this. Let's find a place where we can talk and gather our allies…"

Ara nodded in understanding and waited for him to sidle past her towards the open door. His taloned feet stepped into the corridor and with a look back at Ara he stretched his wings to their fullest before lifting off.

Ara and Tobias made their way slowly through the tunnels at first, with Tobias flying a certain distance and then stopping to wait for Ara once the coast was clear.

A few things became apparent as they made their way through the darkness—there were no living souls anywhere in their vicinity save for a few mice, and that something had to be going on elsewhere in the Citadel. They both noted odd winds traveling the mostly stale passages. Ara had a guess as to what it might mean but kept quiet so they both could concentrate.

At the next intersection, Tobias drew abreast of the wall and motioned for Ara to join him. It had grown steadily lighter in the past few minutes, and Ara guessed they were nearing the main lower levels of storerooms and places where people might be wandering about, attending to the business of the day—or night. Ara knew that it was only a matter of time before they ran into someone.

"I sense a being just ahead," Tobias said. *"Let's proceed slowly here."*

Ara nodded to him and they peered around the corner together, Ara crouched at his level. A set of iridescent jade eyes flashed back at them from down the hallway.

"Buster!" whispered Ara hoarsely to the cat. She watched in delight as his back arched and he trotted down to meet them.

Tobias extended his wings to appear larger. Buster meowed as he drew near Ara's outstretched hand and rubbed his head against her fingers in greeting. He eyed the giant hawk with what Ara thought to be a mixture of interest and superiority.

"Hi, old friend," Ara murmured softly, as Buster began to purr.

Ara knew Buster's presence signaled they were getting closer to the main core of the Citadel. While Ara and Buster got reacquainted, Tobias took the opportunity to scout out the rest of the hallway.

A long look passed between bird and cat.

"He is showing me images of the day," began Tobias thoughtfully.

"Oh! I remember, he did that for me once, too. What do you see?" she asked.

"There is some kind of commotion above, with people running around. He's showing a being with large wings... And it seems that he sensed you were near, and was looking for you," Tobias continued.

"Ixytria!" Ara exclaimed. Tobias gave her a funny expression. "I'll explain more as soon as we find the right spot," Ara added.

"Indeed—and I need some camouflage. Let's see if we can find a laundry room on the way."

Tobias and Buster exchanged another long glance, after which Buster stretched his front paws, shook himself, and set off at a trot down the hallway.

Buster led Tobias and Ara past a series of storerooms to an unlit laundry room where Ara took a moment to rummage through bins holding a torch. After locating a suitable robe for herself and Tobias, they swiftly made their way to the upper levels of the Citadel, where it soon became obvious that it was nighttime.

Ara learned as they went that Tobias preferred them to enter the Great Hall at midnight, or close thereafter. It was their best chance to enter unseen, and the Keeper's power along with the Dark Spirit's would be at its most potent then.

When Ara questioned this approach, Tobias simply answered, *"They will also be at their most arrogant and apt to make a mistake, Ara."*

Only once did they meet other humans on their trip—a set of two guards lounging at a small table before a storeroom of ale. They looked up as a cat, a very large hawk, and a girl passed them by. Ara heard Tobias squawk and wave a wing discreetly to the side. Suddenly uninterested, their gazes returned fixed to the cards each one held in his hands.

At last, they found the ideal room tucked down an empty corridor on the main floor, close enough to the Great Hall but far enough to be private, complete with a cold hearth and multiple time keeping instruments. Buster followed them, making himself at home on a couch.

Tobias circled the room until he found the right place to perch. Ara noted the time before taking a seat on a chair nearby. It was close to ten—they didn't have much time to wait until midnight.

"Tell me, Ara. Tell me everything you can share," said Tobias.

Ara told Tobias of her journey, keeping her tale as brief as possible. It felt so good to share with someone who actually understood. She described her escape through the Treeways, how she'd been caught by the World Tree, meeting Naia and then Ixytria, who had helped to free him. Tobias the hawk was still the entire time, his eyes closed.

"And Naia showed me the truth about this necklace. It's not a stone, like I always thought..." she said, pulling the necklace over her head. She was happy to see that it glowed clearly in the darkened room, and Ara felt a surge of hope as Tobias's eyes widened.

"The Flaming Seed!" Tobias exclaimed. She held it out in a cupped palm for him to look closer.

"From something so small..." he whispered. *"It's a true wonder."*

Tobias tilted his head as if listening to something only a hawk could hear, and then continued. *"We are doubly blessed, Ara. Ixytria has created the path for us to expel the Dark Spirit, and for you to relight the Flame safely, from the ashes as it were,"* he declared.

Ara couldn't have agreed more, though she still couldn't imagine how it would all work.

"While I was down below, I connected with a few who are sympathetic to our cause. I'm afraid the tally isn't large, but I managed to find

some professors and staff who have open hearts and were skilled enough to hear my voice."

Tobias listed the names he'd gathered, stating that he wasn't positive on the details, and Ara smiled when he said Jana's name.

"Describe your friends to me, and how to find them. I don't know if they'll trust a hawk that wakes them in the night, but it's worth a try. We need as large a group as possible to draw the Keeper out and confront him," he said.

Ara had been about to insist that he drink the water from the Sacred Well and change back into his usual form, but this path made more sense. He could fly at liberty through the halls of the Citadel, silent as an owl at night. Ara did her best to describe her friends and the layout of the dormitories. When she'd finished Tobias added one request.

"Send me an image of their energy signature, Ara. One that will carry through the walls."

In that moment, Ara realized that she understood what he meant and sent Tobias an orange dragon for Ember and a blue horse for Nat.

"I see," was his only reply before he stretched his wings and hopped to the floor.

He got as far as the door before he stopped. *"I hear a cart in the hallway."*

Ara edged closer to the door. It was closed but she could see through the keyhole into the hallway. A professor wouldn't push a cart—but maybe someone from the kitchens might.

Ara kneeled on the floor and wedged her face beneath the doorknob until she had a decent view of the corridor.

Moments later, the figure of a girl came into view. She had her hair under a kerchief and was wearing a long white apron. Ara smiled as she caught a clear glimpse of the girl's face as she resettled the platters, her eyebrow raised archly.

It was Ellie!

Ara watched her stop a few doors down and enter a room.

She returned a few moments later carrying a tray. The hallway was silent save for her moving dishes.

"Tobias—I know her! We work in the kitchen together!" Ara whispered.

"Excellent. If you trust her, tell her the plan. But be quick, Ara!" he whispered back.

Ara made up her mind. She waited until Ellie had everything in place and was heading back down the hallway.

"Ellie!" Ara whispered.

She watched as Ellie stopped and turned around.

Ara opened the door a crack and stuck her head out. Ellie's jaw dropped and Ara desperately gestured for her to remain quiet.

She abandoned the cart and scurried over to join Ara. "What—are you doing?" she whispered loudly. "And where have you been?" she said, wide eyes searching Ara's face.

Ara wanted to give her a hug. "I am so happy to see you! And I don't have time to explain anything right now... Are you heading back down to the kitchens?" she asked.

Ellie rolled her eyes. "Yes—I was just bringing food up for an emergency meeting tonight in the Keeper's quarters and I'm already late going back. There's just too much going on right now, wait till you hear," she started.

But Ara headed her off. "Good—tell Geera and everyone there to come up to the Great Hall at midnight. And not a moment before! I think I'll need your help."

Ellie stared back at Ara for a few seconds and Ara saw her keen eyes take in the Greenspell coiled tightly at her wrists.

"You're dead serious! Ok, I will... Geera is already in a fuss over the rumors of dragons, and the Flame going out—and an army somewhere, too. It's been chaos! I don't know who will still be up, but I'll let everyone know," she agreed.

"Thanks Ellie!" Ara whispered, already closing the door.

Ara wasn't exactly sure what she had just set in motion, but she knew Ellie could be trusted to relay the message. She knelt before Tobias on the floor and told him about her exchange with Ellie.

"Good—the more people the better. And a meeting sounds like an added bonus," he replied.

He waddled to the door and looked at Ara. *"Now can you open the door?"*

Ara stuck her head out to scout the hallway then opened it wide enough for him to jump out.

"I'll return soon!" he called back as he flew down the hall.

Ara sent a silent prayer that he would find everyone who could help and wouldn't be caught again.

Ara paced the room. Would anyone come? And what if it were just herself and Tobias, alone? Could he hold both the Keeper and Dark Spirit at bay while she relit the Flame?

Ara went to sit with Buster and pulled out the Seed from beneath her sweater to study its light. The room was still dark, but Ara could see the hands of the clock on the mantel.

A few minutes later there was a soft knock at the door, and then a figure peered in. Ara's heart leapt as she took in Jana's bewildered expression. She was in her nightgown and her hands clutched a shawl at her shoulders. She peered around the room as if looking for someone and then sped to Ara.

"Ara, dear! Are you alright?!" she cried softly, and Ara let herself be enfolded in her warm embrace.

"I'm okay! And I'm so happy to see you, Jana!" she whispered back.

"We were so worried that you were lost in a Shadow Storm! There are still teams of hunters, out looking for you," she said, and gave Ara another squeeze.

Ara realized that she had been missing for over a full day, though it felt like she'd been gone a lifetime.

Agatha was the next to arrive. Ara ran to her and they had a quiet exchange—Agatha had seen a great bird who'd spoken to her, and she knew she needed to come.

"His name is Tobias, and he should be here soon," Ara answered to Jana and Agatha both.

Before they could ask Ara what was going on, Tobias flew into the room, followed by Ember and Nat. Ember muttered something about a party and Ara ran to hug him as he was sizing up Tobias and taking in the presence of Jana and Agatha.

"You came, it worked!" Ara nearly cried. Ember returned her hug and let go quickly.

When Ara hugged her Nat held on for longer and whispered, "We were getting worried!"

"And where have you been—for real?" Ember asked.

"I know, I'm sorry…but I made it to the World Tree! It's a long story and I can't wait to tell you," Ara whispered back.

A few new faces arrived next, including people on the staff in overalls and one lone professor that she'd never seen before. Ara looked at the growing crowd, and then over to Tobias who stood awkwardly next to the couch.

"And who is he?" Nat whispered.

"I think this is everyone Ara. Can you tell them that I'll be with them shortly? And bring your waterskin and the robe we found earlier. I'll head to that closet over there," Tobias said, gesturing with a wing to a door Ara hadn't noticed before.

"Okay—good idea," Ara replied.

She gave a brief explanation stating that Tobias was a man and a Shaman who had once been a Scholar, and then followed him to the closet. She noticed Agatha speaking quietly with Jana.

"Okay, here's everything," Ara said, passing the water and robe into the dark closet.

Ara realized that Tobias couldn't open the water by himself and made sure that he could drink it easily with his beak. He spoke softly before she turned to let him undergo his metamorphosis in peace.

"I don't know how long this will take, or what I will undergo, Ara… Let's hope it's only a few minutes. But if something goes wrong, continue

on. You have support all around you," he said before closing his golden eyes.

Ara shut the door and backed away. When she turned around there were many sets of eyes looking at her; most in bewilderment, but a few with understanding.

Ara walked to the couch where Nat and Ember were seated and sat on the floor. The room was silent and Ara realized that she had better start preparing her explanation of what was happening, and what was to come. Even though she hadn't figured it out yet.

And then the door to the closet creaked open. No one else had ever seen Tobias the person before, and so they didn't know what to expect. But Ara jumped up, almost forgetting that they needed to be quiet. Tall and radiantly healthy, he looked like a young man ready to be raised to a Scholar. His long dark braids hung freely at his shoulders and his face was no longer lined. Ara's jaw hung open at the change. Only his eyes were truly the same—like a hawk's.

"Tobias!" cried Ara. Beside her, Ember let out a low whistle.

"Yes," he said, a smile in his voice. He held his hands up to the light as if seeing them for the first time.

"You look so much younger!" Ara exclaimed.

Tobias laughed back at her as he walked from the closet and bowed to the onlooking group. "Thank you for your patience. That was an unexpected miracle," he said, and Ara thought that even his voice had changed.

Glancing around the room she could see the effect of his quiet power. No modern Scholars were shapeshifters, let alone dreamwalkers like the hawk that had visited them from its captivity.

Jana stepped forward and spoke to Tobias. "I am happy to see your face in person," she said, bowing. "And thank you for protecting her."

"As am I. Far more than you know. I take it you understood my broader messages," Tobias asked.

Jana sighed. "I did... In fact, I think I might have sensed that things were amiss—but I didn't realize the full scope of the Keeper's plans. You mentioned his army at the World Tree, and just earlier today someone saw him return in a velocraft dressed in a commander's uniform. That was the outer confirmation I needed," she replied.

Ara was about to tell Jana that she had been with him in that same velocraft, but bit back the words as Tobias addressed the group.

"I honor each one of you for coming to help. I'm sorry that I haven't been able to fully convey the nature of what is wrong. The essence is this—there is a very powerful Dark Spirit in the Keeper's body. It gives him extra powers, which he is now abusing in his battle for the World Tree. I understand there was a commotion in the Great Hall today. Can anyone report what happened?" Tobias asked.

"There was a dragon in there! A great blue dragon that made it rain. I saw it as I walked by with a group of friends, before they shut the doors!" piped Ember. Tobias nodded to him.

Jana tilted her head, but basically supported Ember's account. "I was told by Professor Nirla that a demon had caused trouble in the hall. But it is true that water was everywhere, and a whole team was sent to clean up. Some said the Flame is out, but we can't be sure," she said.

"I was on the clean-up crew. And it's true about the Flame, I'm very sorry to say," said the man in overalls. "We tried for hours to contain the water. It's no longer raining inside, but there's still a cloud with a shaft of light falling from it. It's like it leads to a sky in another world," he said.

Tobias bowed his head in thanks. "This is our goal. We need to get the Keeper to stand in that shaft of light," Tobias said firmly, golden eyes aglow.

Ara watched the faces of her friends and teachers. The older ones nodded, as if to themselves, and the younger ones looked incredulous. A number of people began to ask questions at once and Tobias quieted them again.

"This has already been a matter of life and death. Ara here just rescued me from the dungeons," he said, gesturing with a hand to Ara.

She noted the looks of surprise ripple about the room, but no one spoke.

"And if the Keeper is successful at the World Tree, he will be given immortal life. We should enter the hall close to midnight, by my estimations. We now have less than an hour. I suggest we speak only of what we wish to accomplish."

The tone of Tobias's words shifted the entire conversation to strategy. Agatha recounted the finer points of the entrances to the hall and Jana spoke of the Keeper's late-night habits. Ara herself chimed in with the information on the nighttime meeting. It was agreed that they would enter the Hall in two groups, one large and one small. The larger one for luring and engaging the Keeper and the smaller one to give Ara cover at the Flame— or whatever was left of it.

"And what are *you* going to do?" Ember asked her.

She hadn't expected to say her plan out loud. She looked at Ember and Nat, standing to either side of her. There was so much she wanted to tell them, but it would have to wait. Their clear and steady gazes told her how much they trusted her. Then she looked to Tobias.

"Why don't you show everyone, Ara?" he said.

"I'm going to relight the Flame," she said, drawing the Flaming Seed from around her neck, "with this."

Ara held out the Seed in her hand, glowing clearly in the darkened room. She heard soft gasps of wonder, and Agatha said, "Blessed be!"

"It's from the World Tree. I was just there, and I saw the battlefield...and everything," Ara said in the quiet.

"Wow...so you were really there?" whispered Nat, looking at Ara with awe. Ara nodded.

Nat looked into her eyes, questioning. "Is there anything I can do? We can do?" she asked.

Ara could tell how much she wanted to help. "I don't know yet...but, I don't think so."

Saying the words made her feel bad, but Nat nodded, as if she understood.

Ara replaced the necklace and gave it a soft pat. Now that everyone had seen it, she could feel the group had grown closer. Jana kept giving her warm but curious glances.

Ember sidled over to her and whispered, "Well, we always knew you were weird..." Ara smiled back at him.

When it was just a few minutes before midnight, Tobias turned to Ara. "I think we should go now—are you ready, Ara?" he asked her.

Ara looked up into his eyes, shining with tenderness and respect. "No...and yes!" she replied.

Tobias gave her a solemn nod. He then turned to Buster, with whom he had a rapid exchange. The cat arched his back and then shot towards the door.

"It's time..." Tobias announced to everyone.

There was a rustling of furniture as the small group assembled at the door, and then they were out.

The group made their way through the hushed corridors to the Great Hall as Buster bounded along before them. They skirted the main entrances until the cat drew abreast of a side door that Ara had never noticed before.

Tobias studied it quickly and said something under his breath. He reached out a hand and turned the knob, only to find that it was locked. Ara watched in growing alarm as he waited silently for a few moments, and then turned it again. He pushed the door open a few inches and turned to her.

"The entire Hall is heavily guarded with spells—but it's no matter now. Once we go in, I'll open the largest doors and windows," he whispered.

"Okay!" Ara whispered back.

She could feel power building around them once again, and an equal force of menace push back.

Ara entered behind Agatha and blinked around at the cavernous Hall, now mostly in shadow. It was partially lit in even intervals with warm glow lights and even flickering candles, creating pools of light on the floor. But at the opposite end there was a strange glow in the air, lower than the vaulted ceiling, coming from a small white cloud. A series of ladders and tarps lay scattered beneath it.

"Look! There's water running around the hall," whispered Nat, pointing down at the trough filled with water from Ixytria's storm.

"Could anyone help me with this door?" whispered Tobias from somewhere off in the Hall.

Ara and Ember left Nat with Agatha and found Tobias at one set of the massive doors. He held a giant lever with both hands and gestured with his chin to a button at the side of one door.

"Can you push that as I pull this down?" he whispered.

After some fumbling, Ember found the button, and Tobias was able to pull the last lock free. He then pushed both doors open, the sound of metal on stone rasping in the air. It sounded like they hadn't been opened in years. If that didn't alert the entire Citadel to their presence, Ara didn't know what would.

Tobias stood back for a moment, admiring his handiwork. "These are the east-facing doors—when the sun rises eventually, its light will fall in corners that haven't seen natural light in some time," he said in explanation.

The midnight bells chimed in the distance. Ara didn't need to see Tobias's eyes to feel his intention. He began to walk to the far end of the Hall as the sounds of footsteps and movement traveled to meet them.

Ara, Nat, Ember and Agatha walked behind him and Ara could feel Tobias's powers build, like a golden wall around them. Shapes of faces and people began to come into focus ahead. Were they guards or allies?

The Keeper purposefully cleared his throat and glanced around the long oval table. He sat in his favored spot at one end so he could see the slightest changes of expression in the faces of those around him. Not that he needed to see their faces to know their thoughts. But tonight, he had convened both the Inner and the Outer Councils, which was a first at this dark hour. He needed the Outer Council to feel a part of their next endeavor and sign off on his requests.

After concluding his welcoming remarks, he noted with pleasure that all eighteen of them were on edge and filled with anxiety. He would be happy to put their fears to use.

"Today we at the Citadel have suffered a mighty blow. I'm sure you have heard many rumors of the day's events, but the truth is this: a demon from deep in the mountain extinguished the Flame in a torrent of water," said the Keeper with a somber air.

His words were met with gasps and some groans. Clearly, they had heard at least part of the story already.

"Fear not, he continued. "The Hall is secure, and order has been restored. But now we have the added duty of relighting the Flame. Make no mistake—this was direct interference in response to some very positive news I have to share as well," he said.

"But, sir! How can we relight the Flame? Is it not necessary to maintain connection to the World Tree?" asked a worried member of the Outer Council.

The Keeper couldn't have asked for a better question. "We relight the Flame with a seed from the World Tree, my friend. This practice was passed down to me from the Keeper before," he explained. "As many of you know, we have been more than instrumental in pushing the boundary of Amethys to the south-west, into Onea. Our efforts have finally borne fruit—" the

Keeper paused for maximum effect—"and our forces have overtaken the World Tree."

The Keeper enjoyed the shiver of excitement that swept along the table. A few people from the Outer Council gasped—this was utter news to them—while those on the Inner Council smiled with relief and quiet satisfaction.

"This is a most precious undertaking, as you all are aware. It goes far beyond the relighting of the Flame, which we shall do straightaway. But now we may fully understand the greater architecture of life on Earth. Each species must be documented; every living system dissected and understood. We will hold the tools, and the power—of creation itself."

A hushed moment of awe swept through the group as everyone digested the magnitude of his words. The Keeper pressed on, knowing they would soon forget what he had just spoken aloud.

"But first, we must figure out how to access its powers. It is likely true that it holds the promise of eternal life. Mysteries such as these should remain in the hands of the wisest among us in the Order, as I think you'll all agree. I hold here a proposal for the building of a sufficiently large drill to access the center of the Tree. And we will need more resources to complete this job. This will be uncharted territory for us, and I hope that everyone is as thrilled with this prospect as I am," he said, holding his papers aloft.

"Our purpose there in now twofold. We can relight the Flame and expand our knowledge. I believe this is divine providence," he said, leaning back in his chair. He could see from the expressions around the table that they believed him without question. And why not—he had spoken the truth save for one lie about the dragon.

The Keeper steepled his long fingers and swept the faces at the table. He watched as bit by bit, they warmed to the idea of the World Tree under their explicit control. Some were already plotting and scheming.

A few lone voices from the Outer Council expressed their concern or skepticism but were no match for his uncanny powers of persuasion. The Keeper pounced on these poor souls as a cat on stunned mice. Was not the advance of knowledge inevitable? Would they not blame themselves afterwards if they had stood idly by while a more powerful nation proceeded to do the same? A nation that might work for selfish ends rather than for the greatest good, as they would most certainly do?

Once this was accomplished and the table happily chatting away, the Keeper let his attention return to his proposal. Perhaps he should request more personnel for the battlefield.

"*Thank you, thank you!*" crowed the Dark Spirit in his ear. The Keeper shifted in his chair.

"*I knew you'd bring her back!*" It sang.

"*What on earth are you speaking about?*" responded the Keeper, but already the blood had begun to drain from his face.

"*The girl! She's in the Great Hall... Oh, thank you!*" It crowed.

The Keeper bade the Dark Spirit to stay with him and felt his limbs go cold. Could she have survived such a fall? The possibility was so alarming it caused him to stand.

"Please excuse me, friends. You are welcome to stay here and chat as long as you wish, but I have a few things to attend to before resting... As you know, my health is still on the mend," he said calmly.

When others began to get up, he gestured them to sit. Thankfully, they were all unaware of the time and the discussion was still in full swing.

"Please continue without me if you feel called to this work," he added, shooting a quick glance at his closest circle as he crossed the room with lengthening strides. One by one they rose discreetly from the table to follow him down to the Great Hall.

＊ 13 ＊

Tobias slowed his steps only when they were in position before the podium. Ara frowned, studying the strangely empty space before turning her attention to the small group standing at the main entrance, now making its way towards them.

The sound of the massive doors being banged and jostled shook the Hall before another small group entered from the doors Tobias had unlocked. Her spirits rose when she saw Geera, Ellie and dear Henry in the lead. Ara's head whipped about between the three groups, soon to converge in the middle. She instinctively reached for a nearby hand as she saw the Keeper stride forward, electric with power.

In the next second, all of the doors to the Great Hall slammed shut and locked from within on their own accord. Ara watched as Henry slowed at the recognition, and then sped up once more. Jana's voice rang through the Hall, closing the distance between the three groups.

"We are here for answers, sir!" she called forcefully, her face trained on the growing form of the Keeper as he began to emerge from the shadows of the Hall.

There was a hush and the sound of approaching footsteps as the Keeper, flanked by five other professors, pressed forward.

"And I am here to maintain order," answered the Keeper with an icy calm.

Ara looked up to Tobias, who stood next to her, in deep concentration. "Now?" she whispered to his profile. He shook his head ever so slightly.

They had maybe a handful of seconds before the three groups met. Jana's group had slowed a fraction in response to the menace in the Keeper's voice. Perhaps now, they too could feel that it wasn't his own.

Ara turned to Nat and Ember beside her. She motioned for them to join Jana and Agatha, and they quietly fell back. Ember turned around partway, and Ara gave him a tiny wave. She could barely wait any longer. She looked back to Tobias and watched as his golden eyes narrowed ever so slightly.

"Go now! I will stand guard—no one will disturb you. And I will be here, waiting, when you return," he said.

Ara tore herself away and ran the remaining steps to the empty platform. Her right foot hit the first step of the dais just as the Keeper bellowed, "Stop her!"

Ara heard footsteps and the sound of a scuffle behind her but didn't slow until she was right before the blue chalice, sitting like a forgotten relic.

More shouts rang through the Hall as the three groups became one. Tobias's voice rose above all else as he called out a phrase in an ancient language, like a cross between a song and a battle cry, and Ara grabbed the chalice.

She settled herself in the place that felt best, kneeling on the floor. She needed to concentrate now, above all else. Doing her best to block out the sounds of voices and scuffles, she sent out a silent prayer that all would be well and focused on calming herself. She removed the Flaming Seed from its fastening in the necklace and placed it carefully in the cup where its golden light shone brightly.

Ara closed her eyes and called upon the Greenspell. With the vines floating above her skin, their light seemed to blend with the light from the seed. She touched it gently and whispered, "*Grow!*"

A tiny golden flame leapt to life.

"*Grow!*" Ara whispered again, and it doubled in size at the sound of her voice. A smile began to form on her lips.

Now it was an inch high, floating above the Seed.

"Grow!" Ara said, more loudly this time.

The Keeper shifted his concentration a fraction to the right. If his energies and those of his chosen group could form a triangle, he wouldn't need to move. In fact, he could stay locked in this embrace with Tobias for a decade. It was six to one, and only Tobias would weaken over time. The man was doing his best to drag him into the portal while being ensnared in a very powerful spell from the Inner Council.

The Keeper held his ground. From a distance it probably looked like two friends embracing after a long time apart. Tobias's singular eyes refused to look into his own, his face turned towards the golden light, now trickling down from the portal several feet away, and still far too close for the Keeper.

He checked on the bystanders quickly to make sure no one had moved... Not that they could, anyway. The Dark Spirit had overstepped Its bounds, pushing each person against a wall and covering their mouths with air to keep them silent.

The Keeper noticed that the guard, Henry, was still trying to grasp the long knife buckled at his waist—as if that would help. He would have preferred to shepherd them out of the Hall with assuring words, but once the girl had climbed on the podium it was too late for such niceties.

They now had only minutes to regain control, and so he hadn't tried to stop the Dark Spirit when It flew out from his field. That was when Tobias had charged him, as if he'd seen the change in real time. The Keeper had been shocked by his presence and power, unable to believe what he was seeing until Tobias had knocked him to the floor. Looking into those golden eyes up close, burning with a holy fury, the Keeper had known they were equals in every way.

The Keeper observed a bead of sweat run down the side of Tobias's neck. On the other side of the Hall, the girl sat hunched over the blue chalice, her face glowing in the light.

The Keeper felt a sense of exultation from the Dark Spirit, clamoring to be free. It released itself from the Keeper's field with a howl, and Tobias winced while the Keeper dug deeper into position. Two could play at this game—he'd fought his old friend before and still remembered how.

Ara shrieked as a sharp wind joined her on the podium and circled madly around the floor, interrupting her work. She crouched down and cupped her hands around the little Flame to protect it from the foul darkness that descended around her. The Flame sputtered in her hands as the wind whipped about, faster and faster and a hissing sound grew in her ears.

Red eyes bored from an angry, ghoulish face above her. Ara cowered down.

"At last...you came," hissed the Dark Spirit, with the sound of two rocks rubbing together.

Ara recognized Its voice from the Shadow Storm.

"Thank you for bringing what I asked for, all along," It continued, as It loomed over her.

Ara felt something cold touch her back. It was the same sensation she'd had before she fainted before the Flame. She instinctively jumped up as she felt something come free.

The Dark Spirit had extended Its two claw-like hands to the sky, where It held her wings, streaming with light. Turquoise and gold, they fluttered and glowed in the air.

Her stomach lurched as Ara understood what had just happened. "You can't take my wings!" she cried.

Even if they were invisible to everyone else, she could see them now—and they were real!

"But I already did, you see... They're the ideal building blocks for what I need. Such perfect particles of light," rasped the Spirit.

Ara backed away as far as she dared, hands still protecting the tiny Flame.

The Dark Spirit cackled and whirled itself in a circle again around her, before leaving the podium with a final roar.

And the cup held the Seed alone.

Ara looked down at the chalice and collapsed on the floor. Why was this so hard? She broke into tears, exhausted. If Tobias had won, the Dark Spirit wouldn't have been free!

"Get up!" she said to herself, as she lay there in a ball. "You can do this, with or without wings!"

Ara pushed herself up onto her hands and knees. She scooted back into position before the Seed. She'd lost her wings to the Dark Spirit...but maybe they would grow back. And what was it that her grandmother had said—about togetherness?

Ara realized that she had tried to do everything the wrong way. She'd been so focused on her new magical powers that she had forgotten the deeper meaning of what Naia had said.

"*Hesperia? It's Ara... I'm here!*" she whispered.

But was the Guardian still there? And would she be able to come now that the Flame was no more?

Ara closed her eyes and waited. Nothing happened, and the Hall had gone eerily silent around her.

Then a figure of a woman formed beside her. She looked down lovingly at the Seed, and then at Ara.

"*Welcome, Ara. Thank you for invoking me and returning with the Seed. It is now the beginning of a new cycle, and it shall be a new fire that burns here. Why don't you ask the Seed what its wishes are?*"

Ara swallowed and nodded. Of course, she should have asked to begin with. The Seed was connected to the Tree!

With the Greenspell still awake at her wrists, Ara reached out and touched the Seed with a finger. "*Hello, beautiful seed! How can I relight the Flame? Can you show me?*" she asked.

A glowing sense of warmth spread through her chest and then her entire body as the Seed sent her a picture of what it wanted. Ara understood there were no spells, no magic symbols. There was no advanced knowledge that she needed or intricate concepts.

"*Thank you,*" she sent, and got up from the podium.

The Keeper felt his feet shift forward as Tobias took the opportunity to gain the upper hand while his energies were spread thin. A low growl vibrated from his throat as he pulled him another inch closer to the portal.

Moments later, the Dark Spirit returned to hover just outside of his field.

The Keeper waited with his breath held, as another second passed.

Tobias tugged him forward yet again.

Would the man not give up?

"*I can fashion my own body now...I don't need yours,*" exclaimed the Voice in his mind.

The Keeper felt like a trapdoor had just opened in the floor beneath him, and a hollowness began to form in the pit of his stomach. The Dark Spirit wanted to be rid of him?

Without moving his head, he looked to where It was positioned several feet away. It held glittering wings in Its long, half-formed claws, an expression of rapture on Its face.

Tobias pulled the Keeper a hair closer to the portal and he sensed a thread of alarm from Marlowe, one of his trusted deputies.

"Hold steady," he sent to the five of them, who stood in complete stillness, arranged strategically about the Hall.

And then he addressed the Dark Spirit, busily trying to mold something from the shreds of light. *"I'm afraid that won't work, old friend... You can't make a body from that magical substance—it only adheres to the rules of the Light. You'll need to make do with mine."*

Unbelieving, the Voice railed at him without taking his gaze from his prize. Tobias shifted him another inch forward, and the Keeper started to panic.

If the Dark Spirit didn't return to his body, what then?

The Keeper flashed through multiple possibilities, each one separated by the slimmest margin of choice or error. His natural human form would return, and he would be no more. If the Dark Spirit left his body for good, he might have only days left to live or only minutes. Unless he could get his hands on the sap of the World Tree first.

The highest path forward was clear—he had already lost control of the Dark Spirit once. And something had shifted across the Hall.

The Keeper closed his eyes and sensed a change but couldn't identify what it was. And then he knew—the Guardian was there, and the girl was coming. The girl that would expose him completely.

Grolyn relaxed his energy a fraction so that only Tobias would sense the difference. His old friend seemed to register the change but didn't trust him yet. And why would he?

"I know the commands—help me now with this and I will assist you afterwards," he said to the Dark Spirit in his most calming and authoritative voice.

The Keeper held his breath as the Dark Spirit considered his words. It was very difficult to lie to It, but not impossible. It fashioned the wisps into a ball and placed it out of reach of human arms for safekeeping. The Keeper knew It wouldn't stay long in that form and would fade back into the light from which It originated.

A moment later, he nearly had the wind knocked out of him as the Dark Spirit returned to his body, anxious and ready for battle. He knew he had only seconds to execute this plan—and he needed Tobias.

The Inner Council were exerting all of their power to keep Tobias from moving. It was a miracle the man could even bat an eyelash. But the same wasn't true for him. He was free to run, and that was the last thing anyone—including the Dark Spirit— expected him to do.

The Keeper made his decision and spoke the Dark Spirit's name—the one he himself had forgotten but Tobias had remembered, from the day they had summoned It together. The name came out in long, slow syllables, like a call from the depths.

The Keeper felt the Dark Spirit bind to him, unable to move, Its voice shifting from anger to alarm. It had never been trapped in his body before, and now It was bound by Its name and the Keeper's will.

Grolyn opened a pathway of communication from a long-forgotten part of himself to Tobias. It was the only free channel left, and the only place where the Dark Spirit had never ventured. Closing his eyes, he prayed it would still work.

"I will end this! Let me go! Let me go, now!" he sent from his heart, as he finally made contact with Tobias's heart, the strength of its light like an inferno.

Tobias's eyes searched his own for confirmation, and he must have seen what he needed. He released his death hold from around his body.

Suddenly free, the Keeper shot him a parting look before he ran to the golden light of the portal with all of his power.

Ara froze at the top of the stairs. Five professors stood in an odd formation near the center of the Hall, and everyone else was pinned up against a wall, held there by an invisible force.

Ara searched for Nat and Ember and found them next to each other. Neither one could speak, but Ara could tell they were wide awake. They saw her and she nearly ran to them except something in their eyes told her not to move.

Ara refocused on the portal at the far end of the Hall and the two figures there. One lay on the ground in the shaft of light—could it be...?

Tobias knelt beside the crumpled form of the Keeper. Ara watched from a distance as Tobias gently closed the Keeper's eyes. His gaze lingered on his face for several seconds and then he sat back on his heels, looking up into the portal. And then he turned his eyes towards her.

Ara descended the stairs as if in slow motion, but as she drew closer her quiet steps became a full-on run.

"Ara!" was all he said, as he got to his feet to embrace her. Ara looked up into his golden eyes. "Is the Dark Spirit really—?" she began.

"—gone? Yes, as is my old friend. It was his choice at the end," Tobias said softly.

Ara looked at the soft trickle of golden light and bowed her head.

"And the Flame?" asked Tobias.

"I understand how to light it now...but I need everyone to help," she said.

Tobias smiled down at her. "Well done, Ara. I'll take care of these five for the time being," he said, and gestured with his chin to the Inner Council.

Ara thought they looked a bit worried. Luckily for them, Tobias was kind.

Sunlight had begun to stream into the Great Hall, and the spells holding everyone against the wall had lifted with the Keeper's passing. The light swept across their faces, and it looked like everyone was awaking from a dream.

Ara ran to Nat and Ember, who had just started moving away

from the wall. She hugged them both, and then pulled them with her to the top of the podium.

"I thought I could do this myself—but I can't. I need your help. Will you come up with me?" she asked.

Nat smiled at her. "After all of that? I'll try anything!" she said.

Ember eyed the blue chalice. "Do you still have the Seed in there?" he asked, and Ara could tell he was curious.

"Yes, you'll see. Come!" Ara assured him.

Ara then turned to the group still waking up. "Quick, I need everyone!" she called.

As the sunlight hit their faces, she saw the stunned expressions begin to melt. Agatha blinked at her and then began to walk toward the podium. Jana held back and Ara waved again.

"Please, I can't do it alone! We have to do it together," she said, breathless.

Ara searched for Tobias but saw him hanging back, still holding the five professors in check. He smiled at her, and she understood. This was for them to do.

"Don't be afraid, just go up and sit on the podium!" Ara said as Ellie and Geera approached, dubious expressions on their faces.

"It's okay, Geera," Ara said, placing a hand on her shoulder as she started up the stairs.

At last Henry stood before the podium. He looked from Tobias to Ara. "I don't know, miss..." he said.

"Henry! Please come... Will you take my hand?" Ara asked him. He tilted his head in response and Ara grabbed his large hand and pulled him up with her.

Once they were all assembled, Ara looked at the faces of the group sitting in a circle around the chalice. She took a deep breath.

"When I was at the World Tree, it showed me how all of the Flames around the world are connected. And it said that they're for everyone, not just the Order," she said in a voice that sounded clear and strong in her ears.

"All we need to do is focus on the Seed and send a beam of love from our hearts. I call it a heartbeam. See the light around the Seed as alive and wish for it to grow!" she said.

Ara watched in anticipation as everyone focused on the Seed. She felt the Greenspell tingle as she sent out the strongest heartbeam she could.

Little gasps erupted around the circle as a flame leapt to life from the Seed, shining with an otherworldly light. They were now seeing what the Seed had shown her. Everyone sat transfixed, gazing at the small star that burned where the Seed had been.

Within moments, it had grown to the size of a bonfire. Unlike the old Flame, this one was white with shimmering rainbows, like an opal.

Ara grinned, and felt a tear fall down her cheek as she took in the faces of everyone around her, the opal Flame reflected in each set of eyes.

Something flickered in the center, and for a split-second Ara saw a tiny, wizened face staring back at her, two large insects perched on either shoulder.

Naia smiled and waved to her, and Ara waved back.

Just beyond the circle, Ara saw Hesperia bow deeply.

They had done it—together.

EPILOGUE

Ara sniffed the air—it was soft and held the faintest scent of leaves. She scanned the identical trees around her and set off over the thick carpet of moss. Careful to walk in the tracks she'd made before, she cast her thoughts back to all that had happened, and all that had changed.

Ara had spent the summer at home, enjoying the long, slow days with her family. She'd told them everything she could of her journey and specifically her time with Naia at the World Tree.

Ara had seen a kindling of light and curiosity in the eyes of her parents and a deep recognition in those of her grandmother. Yet they all were amazed that an old family heirloom had been far more than it appeared.

Overall, she had been impressed by how open-minded and thoughtful they were, her grandmother especially—she knew when to ask her questions and when to let her sit in silence as she took in all that had happened.

By the time autumn returned, Ara sensed a change in the

Great Boreal Forest. It was lighter and softer. And when it came time to return to the Citadel for a new year, Ara was ready.

This time both of her parents made the journey down with her and stayed for several days to see things for themselves, and make sure Ara got settled properly. They moved her into a new room and accompanied her nearly everywhere she went. She'd finally had to tell them that she really was okay. And this time, it wasn't an exaggeration.

Ara couldn't believe the changes in the Citadel already. The Inner Council had been replaced by one large Council, which included several new faces from the staff. The office of the Keeper had been abandoned, and a small, thoughtful memorial to Grolyn stood near the entrance to the gardens. There was a feeling of lightness and possibility, and the new Flame seemed to sparkle for Ara whenever she looked upon it.

And eventually, she had made her way to Tobias.

Before leaving the Hall that fateful day, he'd placed a hand on her shoulder and whispered in her ear, "When you're ready, Ara, I'll be waiting," he'd said, before turning to walk freely from the Hall.

Ara hadn't been ready to watch him go, but she'd had her friends beside her, so it had been especially wonderful to bring Nat and Ember to the great tree, Gobo, and have Tobias show them around. Now that the forest was no longer off limits and Shadow Storms a thing of the past, they were able to slip away from the Citadel more easily.

Just like Ara had snuck out today. She'd chatted briefly with Tobias, who'd been working on updating his feathervane in the yard. He'd watched her open the portal tree, where dandelions still grew despite the chill in the air as winter approached.

"I'll give you an hour. If you're not back by then, I'm coming to get you," he'd said with a smile as she passed through into the Treeways.

Ara's steps slowed before the hollow tree that had once held Silwa. She passed a few others just like it until she came to a stop before the tree with three squiggly lines. Ara placed her hands on the bark and watched the golden light shimmer beneath them.

Ever so gradually, the portal opened until it was wide enough for her to enter. Ara could see bright red earth and the sun blazing from a clear blue sky.

Ara thanked the tree, took a deep breath, and stepped through to the other side.

ACKNOWLEDGMENTS

Creating a book truly takes a village, and I am so grateful for all of the support I've received.

Thanks to Lisa Edwards, an extraordinary editor and book shepherd—Namaste, Lisa! Many thanks to the guiding light of M.M., Opie, and Ashley in the writing process. A huge thank-you to all my family and friends who were patient readers of the many versions of this story—Heidi, Rita, Lee, Karabelle, Laura, Guy, Sophia, my father, Jesse, and especially my mother, Alice, who read nearly every questionable draft—thanks, Mom. And thanks to all of my quiet champions who urged me to keep writing. Thank you to all of my teachers over the years—Djuna, Siobhan, Nan, Marguerite, Sandy, Kim, Jennifer, Xi, Simmin, Nancy, and the goddess group in Philadelphia.

I'd also like to acknowledge the work of the late Dagara Elder, Maldioma Somé of Burkina-Faso, my ancestors, and the ancestors native to the land on which we live in northern Vermont. And lastly, my beautiful husband, Brad, and our magical daughter, Elora. You have my infinite love.

ABOUT THE AUTHOR

Sybil grew up in Burlington, VT, and often played the bard at sleepovers, keeping her friends awake with spooky stories and tales from mythology. After attending Harvard College, she chose the path of greatest resistance and became a ballet dancer, enjoying a nearly twenty-year career dancing in four companies in the US and abroad. Sybil enjoys all things mystical and lives with her husband and daughter in northern Vermont.